Murder and Homicide X

Peter J. Michael

Murder and Homicide X

ISBN-13: 978-1-923666-30-6

Published by Peter J. Michael

ALL BOOKS BY THIS AUTHOR ARE:

THE GREAT WAR AGAINST
TERRORISM

KILLING THE BOGEYMAN I & II

RUTHLESS

RELIGIOUS DEATH TRAP

THE GOD OF ELIMINATION

THE MURDEROUS MR. A

MADMAN'S RETURN

MURDER AND HOMICIDE I - X

Part 'ten' of the Murder and Homicide cops versus villains' fiction book series.

Murder and Homicide X

MURDER AND HOMICIDE X

CHAPTER 1

Robert Stewart noticed the shifty guilty flickering eyes staring back-and-forth towards him that afternoon by his main targets. The obvious appearance of dishonesty by such people who wore titles in society as so-called reputable and respectable individuals, was irritatingly apparent to him by such despicable and disgusting hypocrisy his targets had worn as dirty clothes, that exuded every inch of their filthy characters from their heads, all the way down to their feet.

Robert Stewart glanced at them with cold deliberate eyes unnoticed, as they were glancing at him with flickering eyes; eyes which were horrendously dishonest in their implications and dire suggestions, that Robert studied and expertly identified as see-through glass.

Robert Stewart gazed at them and noticed they were glancing at him back from a short two-metre distance away. Robert's presence was unexpected on his part. He did not deliberately intend to bump into these targeted fiends. But they so happened, by an act of fateful coincidence, to be close by in his presence and proximity. And by the way they kept staring back-and-forth at him, Robert understood he was the topic of their discussions wholeheartedly. Or to his dismay!

The corrupt hypocrites who wore respected titles attempted to act inconspicuous, but Robert understood their natures all too well. Shit could not hide itself in his presence. He saw through mud, sewer rats and all forms of grime and slime, as if his personal mind's human trash detector of such scumbags, sent out very noteworthy alarm bells every time he was in the proximity of such dirtbags, close by and from a distance!!!

That afternoon, Robert Stewart accompanied his beautiful wife Cassandra for lunch at Sam Cornelli's famous nightclub-restaurant in Brooklyn, New York, when he so happened to notice those filthy and vile people his Police Department office had been targeting, just walking inside the restaurant, possibly by coincidence as well, and seated themselves at a table a couple of metres away. And after they seated themselves down, they noticed Robert Stewart was having lunch inside the restaurant with his wife. And then the back-and-forth stares by the targets towards Robert Stewart began incessantly for several moments, as they commenced whispering words, diabolical words in crosstalk concerning their main subject, Robert Stewart.

Who were the menacing targets that Robert Stewart was eyeballing in curious police investigative scrutinies? The targets comprised of the latest appointed corrupt Brooklyn District Attorney named Dave Glick, a corrupt New York City Judge, named Lou Larsen, a corrupt priest, who happened to be the eldest brother of Elliot Archer, named Vince Archer, and deceased Psychiatrist Steven Archer's wife or widow, also a psychiatrist herself, named Psychiatrist Rue Archer. Robert had all these two-faced, mask-wearing hypocrites under investigation by his police office at the 25th division precinct station house in Brooklyn, New York. He wanted to nail all of them, on the spot.

But what were their crimes? In Robert's current investigation underway against each and every one of them, plenty. He was accumulating the evidence against them effectively and rapidly.

Both the targeted Brooklyn District Attorney Dave Glick and the New York City Judge Lou Larsen were identified as alcoholics and insane gamblers. They betted fortunes at local casinos and always lost. So, they constantly accepted bribes to feed their money-eating habits, in exchange for fixing courtroom outcomes (mostly before such cases reached trial), and acquitting the guilty. And where necessary, sending the innocent up the river in guilty verdicts for an exorbitant price tag.

Robert Stewart had those two closely monitored with every police resource at his disposal, watching them like hawks, whilst accumulating his evidence. Robert Stewart was sick and tired of Brooklyn District Attorney Dave Glick and corrupt New York City Judge named Lou Larsen getting away with messing up court hearings, as if they were incompetent, but more so than just negligent as prosecutor and judge, they deliberately were fixing court case verdicts in exchange for huge sums of money from criminal defendants.

Robert Stewart heard the complaints of his police officers in New York who arrested a dozen criminals within the past two weeks with solid evidence to convict the criminals, only to have such criminals acquitted in a court of law by corrupt District Attorney Dave Glick and the presiding corrupt New York City Judge named Lou Larsen in such cases. Robert Stewart supervised the investigations of his police officers. He studied the substantial accumulated evidence. He knew his police officers gathered enough evidence to have such criminals thrown in prison for so long, that the keys to their prison cells should have been thrown away for good measure. But instead, because of District Attorney Dave Glick and this presiding New York City Judge named Lou Larsen in those particular cases, the guilty who were wealthy in their natures, bought off the corrupt District Attorney Dave Glick and the corrupt New York City Judge Lou Larsen, guaranteeing their freedoms from court via a not guilty verdict and not guilty verdicts. It was a true mockery of justice. Robert Stewart suspected the district attorney and the presiding judge in such cases of blatant and deliberate fraud and corruption instantly without delay, following those not guilty verdicts given by the horrible judge's ruling and the corrupt clumsy prosecuting manner of the district attorney in those cases during the court proceedings, ignoring evidence and twisting and manipulating words, pointing the guilt into directions of shadows, with coerced smokescreens, which in Robert Stewart's mind, became obvious red flags in such cases, that he knew the pattern was set, whereby influential people with money who were arrested by police and tried in courts of law by the district attorney and the judge in question, ended up having courtroom outcomes fixed - and the guilty getting off scot-free. So, as a result of this unacceptable and intolerable corruption within the justice system, Robert Stewart targeted the Brooklyn District Attorney named Dave Glick and the corrupt New York City Judge presiding in such underhandedly fixed cases, named Lou Larsen, for being bribed to fix courtroom outcomes. Robert Stewart was compiling his evidence and gathering every piece of information, from the united collaborators joined at the hip in the justice system's fixed outcomes, to pinpointing safe deposit boxes where such money (bribes) was given to them by all the people defendants that should have been found guilty in court cases, but instead paid them such hefty bribes to have them walk free, before they even were found, as they should have been found, with enough evidence to warrant trials for their crimes.

Robert Stewart not only identified the safe deposit boxes where the bribes were being stashed in forms of cash through his surveillance operations against the judge and the district attorney, but he also investigated the withdrawals of monies from various front-owned bank accounts of the previous arrested police targets, who used such monetary withdrawals sent directly to the safe deposit boxes of the judge and the district attorney in question, for the sole purpose of conspiring horrendously to fix justice system courtroom outcomes, which led the guilty to walk free in such instances. The payments withdrawn had matched patterns of payments received in directly designed premediated arrangements and police witnessed correlations, implicating all parties involved - and identifying to police investigators of the diabolical fix that was being run rather diabolically within the four walls of the justice system!

So, in short, Robert Stewart was establishing solid proof that the district attorney and the specific judge were deliberately blowing certain cases during courtroom hearings, before such cases were able to reach trial, to end the punishment of the guilty then and there! Also Commander Robert Stewart established the evidence that as the cases were being blown by what should in fact have resulted in guilty verdicts of guilty defendants; the cases chosen by the district attorney and the particular judge in question to be manipulated and sinisterly fixed in their outcomes, were organised towards criminal defendant people who had considerable wealth in their possessions. Consecutively, Robert Stewart traced secret money withdrawals of the defendants' bank account records matching deposits made into specific safety deposit boxes front owned by the district attorney and the judge in question. Robert Stewart knew that the Brooklyn District Attorney and that New York Judge were both rotten apples operating loosely, which led to serious corruption being committed within the walls of the justice system. And their corruption was motivated by monetary greed. They used their bribes to live lavish lifestyles, purchasing expensive cars and buying expensive clothes, at the same time as feeding their gambling addictions in local casinos across New York City, all at the expense of justice being served; and causing police officers efforts to nail guilty criminals much frustration, much annoyance and much setbacks in crucial investigations to have dangerous criminals taken off the streets!!!

Robert Stewart had their entire lives under surveillance. He even watched the district attorney and the judge during the nights they spent together at upscale gambling casinos in Manhattan. And putting two-and-two together, Robert Stewart was able to figure out how they obtained the money to make such large extensive bets in such casinos, when they were being paid to throw court cases of guilty defendants into the toilet, in exchange for such exorbitant payoffs (bribes) they received to gamble large sums of money away, as if their sources of incomes (dirty money) entering their hands from unending sources, had never dried up.

Robert Stewart had the judge and the district attorney under complete surveillance. He had their houses monitored. He even had the district attorney's office under surveillance, as well as the judge in question listened to inside his judge's chambers, when Judge Larsen was situated inside all alone with his criminal collaborators he was in cahoots with, specifically District Attorney Dave Glick.

Robert Stewart listened to everything they said and every sinister act they conspired together to run amok of the justice system. Every dirty act they conspired and every dirty deed they undertook was being listened to and watched by Robert Stewart and his appointed police investigators. Robert Stewart saw with his own two eyes the district attorney and the judge meet secretly together and all alone inside the judge's chambers late at night, having drinks and talking about the next casinos they were going to attend together to gamble all their bribed monetary savings away, within such establishments. He heard the discussions that revealed how flippant they were in doing their jobs properly. But Robert Stewart wanted complete evidence and complete admissions by them of their handiwork, their dirty work they conspired to commit together within the four walls of the justice system, which resulted in guilty people receiving not guilty verdicts or outright acquittals - and leaving courtrooms free like a bird, without ever being found with enough evidence to warrant trials for their guilts. Which, if truth be known, such evidence produced against them by investigating police officers, should have landed them in trial and at the end of that trial, they should have all received guilty verdicts. But instead, because of the corrupt district attorney and the corrupt presiding judge in question operating within New York City, the opposite actually happened. The guilty were found innocent and were acquitted to leave courtroom hearings within minutes, leaving investigative police in attendance at such courtroom hearings flabbergasted, but carefully guarding their emotions from openly confronting the district attorney for his actions of being incompetent, and the judge who ruled unjustly such terrible outcomes, which resulted in criminals of considerable wealth in New York City escaping the justice system, because of those two fraudulent operators (the judge and the district attorney), within the walls of the city's courtrooms. In crux, Robert Stewart was establishing evidence rather fervently that the prosecuting district attorney and this particular New York City judge were accepting bribes to allow vicious criminals and killers get off the hook. Robert Stewart often heard their conversations together indicating how they didn't give a damn if certain people were found not guilty and not convicted during the courtroom cases they were dominating together, in conspired efforts to sabotage the complete workings of the justice system in New York City and New York State! They admitted that those wealthy people they were accepting bribes from would not like it the least if they didn't do their jobs in protecting them and getting them off the hook. And in turn, covering their own arses from being exposed by such bribed individuals of considerable wealth, who may expose the district attorney and the judge to the authorities, if the district attorney and the judge refused to continue accepting bribes from them, to fix courtroom hearing outcomes in the favour of such bribing criminals within the city and state of New York. The district attorney and the judge admitted that they were better served protecting influential men in the city than working against them. Also, they admitted that such people they accepted bribes from were covering for them and protecting them from incurring debts, already accumulated debts, from their gambling losses that even reached certain shylocks throughout the city. So, in short, in a nutshell, Robert Stewart was effectively accumulating necessary evidence that showed District Attorney Dave Glick and New York City Judge Lou Larsen were operating against the law. They were turning the entire justice system's legal process around and upside down, to serve them in their favours, against the community and against investigating police officers who were determined to remove specific dangerous criminals from the streets.

And the judge and the district attorney admitted together that in order to survive and pay their bills and live their lavish lifestyles, they had to know certain things about how the world operates - and they had to protect certain people, which in turn, would result in their own protections by participating in their top-secret favour system. Therefore, in order to remain protected, the judge and the district attorney would admit in conversations together inside the judge's chambers, that they had to close their eyes and close their ears to certain truths about certain people - and just simply let them be and let them get off the hook.

Robert Stewart was quickly establishing the evidence, the damning evidence through his police investigation, that the corrupt Brooklyn District Attorney named Dave Glick and the corrupt New York City Judge named Lou Larsen, had intentionally conspired together to deliberately fix court cases and throw out certain court hearings of certain guilty individuals for money, by such guilty defendants, in exchange to be found not guilty! And Robert Stewart also watched the judge and the prosecutor celebrate in the aftermath of their courtroom disasters they created for police and the community, which resulted in the guilty being acquitted, by drinking whiskey and rum together late at night inside the judge's chambers.

CHAPTER 2

At the same time, as Robert Stewart was accumulating the damning evidence against the corrupt Brooklyn District Attorney Dave Glick and the corrupt New York City Judge named Lou Larsen, via the emotional manipulation used by those toxic people to acquit the guilty, by ignoring evidence and twisting and manipulative words to spin investigative police officers words against them, to shift the blame and craftily bend the truth as powerful strategies, to make the police the problem and the guilty defendants the solution to both the diabolically corrupt district attorney and deviously unscrupulous judge's financial woes, Robert Stewart also was gathering further information and solid proof that a corrupt priest and a corrupt psychiatrist, all in cahoots together with the district attorney and the criminal judge, were collaborating efforts to destroy the entire justice system in New York.

What proof and evidence had Robert accumulated against the priest and the targeted psychiatrist collaborating with the district attorney and the judge in question?

The corrupt priest identified as the eldest brother of Elliot Archer named Vince Archer, was uncovered by the police to have inherited all of Steven Archer's money upon Steven Archer's death. Following Steven Archer's very recent death, the priest became the sole beneficiary since Elliot Archer was in prison or still in jail as it were. So the priest used part of that wealth of millions of dollars by his younger brother Steven Archer, to bribe the prosecutor and the judge to throw out Elliot Archer's case in his upcoming trial; to further acquit the guilty, or at least conspire to, through crucial information Robert Stewart gathered on all of them, their concerted efforts collaborating together to result in imprisoned or incarcerated corrupt ex-cop Elliot Archer, who was guilty of accepting bribes by the Armando family and aiding and abetting in several murders, to let this bastard corrupt police officer walk free. This was the plan derived by Elliot Archer's oldest brother, who inherited all of Steven Archer's money, to use part of that money to bribe the district attorney and the presiding judge in Elliot's case. To fix the courtroom trial he faced, to result in his not guilty verdict and consecutive acquittal, by ignoring all the evidence accumulated against him, so that

Elliot Archer could walk free from court with a not guilty verdict.

Robert Stewart was establishing all the necessary proof and solid evidence against the district attorney, the judge, the priest and the psychiatrist in question, all in cahoots together, deliberately conspiring to make a mockery of the justice system in New York City and New York State!

Robert Stewart also gathered crucial information into deceased Psychiatrist Steven Archer's widow wife, also a psychiatrist named Psychiatrist Rue Archer. Through his police investigation, he uncovered that deceased Late Steven Archer's widow wife, Psychiatrist Rue Archer was also corrupt. She was a psychiatrist accusing Robert of having initiated illegal investigations against innocent people such as her husband Steven Archer, now dead, and also Robert heard through recorded conversations she had over the telephone with District Attorney Dave Glick and Judge Lou Larsen individually, at their homes and private line professional domains, bluntly stating that Robert Stewart was a loose cannon, a slug and a corrupt cop, suffering from her psychiatric diagnosis of Robert's mental condition, she kept repeating over and over and over again, as obsessive-compulsive disorder. She hinted that

Robert Stewart was a very corrupt police commander operating at the 25th division precinct station house of Brooklyn, New York, who should be thrown out of the police force and instead arrested and put on trial for his crimes of trying to prosecute innocent people such as her late husband Steven Archer, and her late husband's younger brother Elliot Archer, currently in lockup in Robert's custody, awaiting trial. Robert Stewart was obsessive-compulsive, obsessive-compulsive, obsessive-compulsive, she kept repeating over and over and over again to the district attorney and judge in separate phone calls she delivered to both of them at night, particularly at their houses on their private phone numbers at various separate occasions.

Robert Stewart tapped the phone calls and was gathering the evidence on all four of the guilty parties comprising of the district attorney, the judge, the priest, and the crooked psychiatrist very neatly and very productively.

Robert Stewart had all of those targets under police investigation. He wiretapped the prosecutor's phone calls, as well as the corrupt judge's phone calls. In addition, he had the same scrutiny imposed against the dirty priest and the evil wicked Psychiatrist Rue Archer at the same time.

So far, Robert Stewart found that the district attorney and the judge presiding over certain judicial cases accepted payoffs to throw courtroom cases of specific wealthy guilty defendants. And now they were accepting bribes by a go-between priest, Elliot Archer's oldest brother named Vince Archer, to throw out Elliot Archer's case and acquit him of all criminal charges, including accepting bribes and conspiracy to murder. Robert Stewart certainly uncovered a hornet's nest quagmire nasty predicament into sordid criminal acts of sabotage and destruction within the four walls of the justice system in New York City and New York State. And the corrupt Brooklyn District Attorney named Dave Glick, the corrupt New York City Judge named Lou Larsen, the corrupt priest, the eldest brother of Elliot Archer named Vince Archer, in addition with the deceased Psychiatrist Steven Archer's widow wife, also a psychiatrist named Psychiatrist Rue Archer, were all in cahoots together, working as a collaborative team, to scheme and scam and slander and sabotage the courtroom legal proceedings and judicial processes in general, case by case, in order to thwart legitimate police officers' investigations and the chain of custody in the handling of evidence against criminal targets and criminal defendants such as Elliot Archer, to have notorious criminals found not guilty, so they could walk free from courtrooms, given deceptive and fraudulent verdicts by this deceptive and fraudulent judge named Lou Larsen, due to the careless and clumsily corrupt and manipulative antics of the District Attorney Dave Glick, so that it would seem legitimately real and not at all conspired, such not guilty verdicts being heinously rendered and unconscionably delivered for the benefit of nasty criminal defendants, as was currently being planned for the upcoming Elliot Archer trial.

Robert Stewart was compiling his evidence speedily, that proved that Brooklyn District Attorney Dave Glick, New York City Judge Lou Larsen, corrupt Priest Vince Archer, and diabolical Psychiatrist Rue Archer were all operating on the wrong side of the law. They were all accepting bribes, in addition to the Priest Vince Archer and Psychiatrist Rue Archer's concerted plans, to now bribe the district attorney and the judge to consecutively throw out Elliot Archer's case, in order to have Elliot Archer, a heinous notorious criminal, exit his incarceration and leave his awaiting courtroom trial proceedings in its aftermath, a free man, to further repeat his offences of accepting bribes and assisting in his conspiracies of further murders.

Robert Stewart planned to get all of them and nail each and every one of them to the wall!!! **As of right now, they were all under investigation!** Robert Stewart even utilised police satellite tracking systems on all of them. He wanted to know their whereabouts at all times, including where they were headed inside their vehicles twenty-four hours of the day! In Robert's mind, he considered all of those perpetrators as detriments to the Police Department! Robert Stewart was adamant that over his dead body would their diabolical schemes succeed! But at the same time, Robert Stewart was aware and prepared that further attempts on his life by these four creeps may further be instigated against him! Robert Stewart took extra precautions in the event that further attempts on his life were in progress!

CHAPTER 3

Right now, at present inside the Sam Cornelli restaurant that afternoon, Robert Stewart noticed from the short-distance positioning of his table a couple of metres away from the four targets, the suspicious gazes going back and forth amongst themselves, and then flickering eyes towards him and back and forth amongst each other again, gossiping words of slander and conspiracies against him, the police commander. Robert sensed their evil intents and wicked whispers!

Robert Stewart had his face towards their table, whilst his wife Cassandra was seated opposite Robert, with her back towards the targets. Robert Stewart had a clear vision of the four subjects. The 50-year-old overweight balding shifty-eyed judge, the 47-year-old slender-built frantic-eyed district attorney, the 48-year-old fat priest and the simple-looking 40-year-old also slender female psychiatrist. They were all eating their expensive meals comprising of lobsters and oysters and drinking expensive champagne, no doubt gossiping about the Commander Robert Stewart at the same time, Robert solemnly interpreted through his scrutinizing gaze of them inconspicuously, as if reading their minds, talking crap about him nonstop!

"That cop Robert Stewart has been responsible for my brother's death. Steven Archer is dead because of Commander Robert Stewart. And Elliot Archer, my youngest brother is in jail because of Robert Stewart. That does not sit with me very well. Not very fucking well at all. I am very, very, very, very, very, very, very, very, angry at Robert fucking Stewart for all that he has fucking done against the Archer family in recent times! My concern now is with my incarcerated brother's release from his confinement. My brother Elliot is suffering due to Robert Stewart's hands! I hope to salvage the situation by working together with all of you to secure his release in his upcoming trial!" Said the corrupt priest eldest brother of Elliot Archer and the older sibling of deceased Steven Archer named Vince Archer.

The judge and district attorney became terrified at Robert Stewart's close by presence and just nodded their heads slightly at the priest's demands, without many words said to that effect, fearing that Robert was perhaps a lip reader, as well as a mind reader, and may interpret their words precisely and accurately, because of his painfully near location and extremely close proximity to them, what with his damn eyesight ability being plunged savagely towards their direction without a moment's notice. After all Robert Stewart was facing them, so he could study them surreptitiously, they considered in their minds, much horrified at the thought!

As soon as Robert finished his brief lunch with his wife Cassandra, he paid the approaching waiter the bill with his credit card, and both he and his wife rose from their chairs and he intended to walk towards the exit past the four united crooks in conspired conversation. Just before he walked past them towards the exit door with his wife, the priest eldest brother of incarcerated Elliot Archer first raised his hand, motioning Robert's immediate attention and yelled out Robert Stewart's name to have him stop before their table. The priest conspicuously wearing his priestly attire and cassock robe he wore everywhere at all times and at every occasion, even when he went to bed, blurted out some smart aleck words to Robert saying, "How dare you Robert Stewart come into this restaurant and have lunch with your wife enjoying yourself, whilst there's so many criminal cases in this city left for you as commander of police to investigate. How dare you, how dare you, how dare you have lunch.

You shouldn't be eating anything until you solve all these criminal cases by all those perpetrators committing all those vile acts which are endangering all our lives," the priest broke out in a smart-arse fashion.

Robert Stewart expected nothing less from these four pathetic crooks but irritating comebacks from them to him. But Robert Stewart remained cool and emotionless as his voice became cold and deliberate to this fiendish priest, when he uttered forcefully strong words, which were intentional but not calculated, but would still land as powerfully as a hammer blow into his guts. Robert Stewart's words were delivered in not so many threats, but certain guaranteed signs that even the idiot he was communicating with would ascertain. "I wouldn't worry about it, Vince Archer. Because I can promise you one thing: lunches or meals or no lunches and meals - all your smart-arse talking and the millions of dollars you inherited from your brother Steven Archer's Will, is not going to help you the least, when I uncover that you are one of those perpetrators in this city committing one of those vile acts. I promise you that Vince Archer! Now try not to choke on your meal!" Robert Stewart said cold as death to the corrupt priest, before he ushered his wife outside the premises and escorted her to her local law firm practise inside his unmarked police car, prior Robert Stewart rapidly making tracks himself to the 25th division precinct station house in Brooklyn, New York.

As soon as Robert Stewart arrived at the Brooklyn Police Station, he stormed inside his office wearing his emotions on his sleeve, rather livid in thought of the smart-arse priest's words towards him earlier. Captain John McCallum and Officer Paul Stewart were already inside Robert Stewart's station house office working on the current police caseloads together, when they noticed Robert's suddenly transparent bad mood he displayed uncontrollably before them.

Robert Stewart shouted at the unpleasant thought of the four hoodlums disguised as honourable people inside the restaurant earlier, "Sons of bitches! Sons of bitches! Sons of bitches!" He repeated out loud angrily.

Captain John McCallum asked very concerned for his police partner's emotional well-being, "what's up Robert? What's the problem?"

Robert Stewart snapped in response, "Vince Archer. Vince Archer, that corrupt priest, that's the problem!"

"What's that scumbag slimy creep done this time?" Asked Officer Paul Stewart curiously.

"I'll tell you what he did!" Blasted Robert Stewart. "I ran into that slimeball earlier down at Sam Cornelli's restaurant, and besides shooting his mouth rather distasteful smart-arse words, he is hinting crap about me taking my wife out to lunch whilst there's so much crime in the city yet to be solved by US police."

Officer Paul Stewart became his usually emotional high-strung self when it came to idiots in the community making deadbeat remarks to the police, "what's that arsehole insinuating? Is he trying to say that the police are not allowed to eat?"

Robert Stewart replied by answering the question with a directed question on his end, yet in a very foul mood at the mere mentioning of that wretched priest's name, "And what exactly is that scumbag priest doing when we're working all through the night and all through the day investigating and solving Major Crimes in the city? I'll tell you what he is doing. He's collaborating with his criminal cohorts that we all have under investigation called, Brooklyn DA Dave Glick, New York City Judge Lou Larsen and Psychiatrist Rue Archer, to dismantle our cases inside the justice system courtrooms' buildings - and have legitimate police cases thrown out of court. That's what those dirty dogs are doing altogether twenty-four hours of the day. Damn I want our police investigation wrapped up soon. I really want to get the goods on all of them with enough ammunition to have them locked up for good - and I emphasise, real soon!" Remarked Robert Stewart anxiously and determinedly to send the corrupt district attorney, the corrupt judge, the corrupt priest and the corrupt psychiatrist all under investigation by his office, into a tightrope noose they would never be able to finagle loopholes in the justice system ever again to escape from!

Robert Stewart insisted on the spot to his police partner Captain John McCallum and his younger brother Officer Paul Stewart, "I want those four broken in pieces! So, what have we got on those lousy slimeballs so far?"

Officer Paul Stewart first blurted out impulsively, "Scumbags Unite!" In reference to their four targets being scene together earlier by Robert Stewart at Sam Cornelli's restaurant. Then Paul Stewart responded to Robert's question of evidence-gathering police tools established so far against the four targets, "we're getting the evidence against all of them at a very good and solid pace. So far, our powerful investigations into the activities of our targets in question, has established evidence of payoffs made by the defendants of serious police case investigations brought before courtroom proceedings, that resulted in charges not sticking, and the acquittals of such major criminals by both the district attorney's blundering performance inside the courtroom (or so he makes it out to believe, to conceal his wilful and deliberate attempts of sabotaging the legal process entirely, through intentional fraud and corruption), whereby at the same time, such courtroom hearings that resulted in fraudulent and deceptive acquittals, were all dominated by Judge Lou Larsen. Also, we're establishing the evidence that Vince Archer, our smart-arse friend, who happens to be a priest in Brooklyn, New York, is conspiring to bribe both the District Attorney Dave Glick and the corrupt Judge Lou Larsen, to get incarcerated corrupt ex-cop Elliot Archer (his youngest brother), off the hook in his approaching trial. So, police investigators are monitoring the situation closely, and as soon as we witness money changing hands, and the detailed discussions of everything that's taking place, as you taught us Robert to be patient in establishing all the evidence necessary, first and foremost, then we move in for the kill and arrest all of them!"

Robert Stewart nodded his head approvingly. His bad mood seemed to have subsided rapidly by this enlightened report from Officer Paul Stewart.

Robert's previously terrible mood had indeed suddenly been alleviated somewhat by his brother, Officer Paul Stewart's assurances, in the police investigation against his four targets at present proceeding rather smoothly. Robert Stewart replied, "excellent. That's exactly what I want to hear. Let's be patient. Let's keep patient for a bit longer, whilst we're hammering into those scoundrels. We're already making headway and establishing a lot of evidence against our targets. Patience is a must to be considered in our investigation. Because I want every piece of information against them. Every clue, every lead. The works. So, we'll just wait until they incriminate themselves further, before we move in to nail all of them to the wall and at the same time! And not a moment sooner!" Robert Stewart demanded to his police collaborators at this present moment in time. Right now, Robert's strategy and his tact was simple: to watch and wait until he obtained every single piece of police gathered evidence against his major targets, to put an end to their courtroom-corruption sprees within the state's courts of law, which ran a complete mockery of the judicial process - and allowed police investigations to lead to dead ends and the acquittals of their targets, by the dirty seeds planted within the walls of the justice system, by the corrupt Brooklyn District Attorney named Dave Glick and his partner in crime, the corrupt New York City Judge, named Lou Larsen!

CHAPTER 4

Robert Stewart carefully watched and listened from a secure distance inside his inconspicuous surveillance van, to his four main targets' evil plots and deplorable schemes being discussed later that evening at 9:30 PM, inside the judge's chambers all alone together, or so they thought.

District Attorney Dave Glick, Judge Lou Larsen, Priest Vince Archer and Psychiatrist Rue Archer gathered inside the judge's chambers, to discuss the intricate details of their plans and the step-by-step nature of how to piece together all the puzzles of their schemes, to continue their lives work of lunacy and insanity, without the intervention of one horribly irritating obstacle in their path, the fundamental stumbling block or outright roadblock, named Commander Robert Stewart.

Their sick and twisted plan comprised of three phases. Phase One: the eradication of Robert Stewart by whatever means necessary. Phase Two: the finagling of the justice system to serve them and them only. Phase Three: accepting a hefty once-off payment from Father Vince Archer, to secure the release of his youngest brother Elliot Archer from Robert

Stewart's custody, by ensuring that the DA Dave Glick and the presiding Judge Lou Larsen in the case, do what they do best during his courtroom proceedings: fix the trial to ensure that incarcerated Elliot Archer escaped prosecution from all his numerous police charges - and was acquitted at the end of his trial, so he could walk the streets freely once again and become entangled in his usual life of crime, which included accepting bribes to aid and abet the powers he served to commit murder and all forms of crimes, with District Attorney Dave Glick and the Judge Lou Larsen covering for him, using their powers within the justice system at every turn.

But first they had to take care of Phase One of their plan. It was not an easy feat to disentangle themselves from this major stumbling block in their paths. The eradication of Robert Stewart by whatever means was still a puzzling task they were racking their brains to try to extricate themselves from such a problem. Because in their minds, without removing Robert Stewart, the rest of their plan's phases may fall through, with Robert Stewart still out there able to cause major problems in the success of each and every one of the main three phases of their current goals. Robert Stewart was not an easy kill in their minds. Not simple to unentangle themselves from! They knew many had tried to eliminate him in the past but failed terribly. Their attempts caused them many losses and many of such perpetrators who plotted the downfall of Robert Stewart, had either ended up in prison or dead or both. So, they had to put their heads together in order to figure out the precise detailed careful strategy of how to deal with the number one obstacle in their way, who was called Commander Robert Stewart.

Judge Lou Larsen considered himself the smartest member of the four-individual group team number gathered inside his judge's chambers that evening, to discuss the success of their three-phase plan. The three-phase plan was after all founded in himself by Judge Lou Larsen. Also, it should be noted that Judge Lou Larsen considered that his judge's chambers was a true safe haven to discuss his criminal plots and wicked schemes he committed for years as judge within the walls of the justice system. Judge Lou Larsen had decorated his judge's chambers luxuriously. He had fine furnishings of expensive genuine leather chairs and marble tables he fixed inside, completely decorating his safe haven chambers in a high-society extravagant fashion. Judge Lou Larsen stood at the corner table of the chambers and poured himself a drink of whiskey and asked everyone gathered inside his chambers if they wanted a drink. They all replied 'yes', so he fixed each of the other three gathered guests a shot of whiskey. And after handing them the drinks, he sat down behind his expensive wooden desk and commenced the discussions as host of the destructive party the gathering could be labelled as, when he would begin communications of his three-phase plan, starting with the most important aspect of that plan, Phase One, which included the removal of Robert Stewart from their lives. Because he noted to all of them, if Robert Stewart, or mentioning him by his title name, 'Commander Robert Stewart' he hinted distastefully, was not removed from the picture, they would no longer be able to continue getting away with their crimes they committed on a daily basis within the justice system's four walls of New York City.

But the fat Priest Vince Archer interrupted his considered 'esteemed colleague' Judge Lou Larsen with the following desperate words he spoke out loud and unhelped, "that fucking cop Commander Robert Stewart is a true menace to us. He has been responsible for the death of my brother Steven Archer. We have to think very hard and put our minds together to figure out the perfect plan to get rid of that cop - or else I promise you all, he's going to be the death and destruction and doom and gloom of the rest of us. We are going to end up all dead in the grave the same way as he killed my younger brother Steven Archer recently!"

Judge Lou Larsen continued as host but kept his calm composure and remained emotionally cool, despite Priest Vince Archer's impatience, and fluctuating cold-and-hot (mostly heated) temperament attitude suddenly flaring up at this time. Judge Lou Larsen spoke freely at this moment whilst he was not being interrupted, "I understand that dilemma we all face with the existence of Commander Robert Stewart in our lives. His existence is a true obstacle to the success of our three-phase plan. Obviously, we cannot repeat the same strategies of trying to murder him as our friend Steven Archer had conspired to commit recently, which ultimately cost Steven Archer and all those he conspired with to assassinate Robert Stewart their lives. Let us not repeat history. We will have to figure out another way to get rid of Robert Stewart. I am a practical man, a pragmatist. We will not adapt, but we will improvise. As a judge operating with the justice system, I know the law. I have been manipulating the law to serve us for years in certain cases. NOW - perhaps the law can work for us as a tool we can utilise to finally get rid of Robert Stewart.

"If we can manipulate court case outcomes and fix courtroom hearings and court trials to acquit certain influential and wealthy individuals, who pay us money to accommodate such bargaining powers for them, perhaps we can manipulate the justice system to work against Robert Stewart. And at the same time, work in our favour! Perhaps we can use the justice system to frame Robert Stewart for certain crimes and get rid of him that way. Because we have to understand, that a second attempt on his life, especially right now, might draw unnecessary heat our way. We have certain people inside this room who are labelled with the Archer surname. It is you people who will be suspected if another hit is attempted against Robert Stewart. And if those very individuals inside this room with that actual surname are implicated, then those associated with you will also be implicated. And that means, me and the district attorney present here this evening! It would become too suspicious, even risky for us to repeat past failures. So, we have to improvise. We have to forgo the errors of our friends of the past and invent new methods and new strategies to deal with this current lunatic loose cannon invading our lives - and causing great obstacles and stumbling blocks in our path, called Robert Stewart. I have some loose ideas in my head of how we can deal with Robert Stewart.

"Perhaps indeed, we can use the law to serve us, and we can use the law to work against Robert Stewart. The very fine ideas I have circulating in my head are in crux, to frame Robert Stewart for certain crimes that will have him removed from his law-enforcement post and law-enforcement posts, so he can no longer come after us and investigate us any further. Because Robert Stewart is a man that many either fear or hate him, because of his attacks against them, putting them out of their criminal businesses and arresting them. So, I say we can forget about putting another price tag on his head via paying someone to eliminate him. Because obviously judging by what happened to Steven Archer recently, that plan failed. So, we have to put our heads together to come up with a better solution, a precise strategy of how we can frame Robert Stewart and set him up for certain crimes, to have him not only removed from the police force, but to have him arrested for life, for such crimes we will indeed set him up for, as guilty of committing. And you District Attorney Dave Glick will certainly relish prosecuting Robert Stewart with such charges we will frame him as the guilty party responsible for committing. And I, as the judge presiding over his case as Judge Larsen, will most certainly enjoy handing him down a guilty verdict, and in turn, sentencing him to either life imprisonment or the death penalty, depending on how well we can set him up as a very serious major criminal in New York City. We have to put our heads together to make him look like a man who has become jealous of people's success, and bitter that he is not in the same financial league as other successful people. So perhaps, we can frame him with bags of drugs in his possession somehow. Perhaps we can frame him for certain murders he will look guilty for committing, even against his own police colleagues, in order to hide his secret life of crime and drug dealing. Let us think about it.

"Perhaps we can arrange for one of Robert Stewart's personal gun weapon revolvers to be taken from his possession with his fingerprints planted all over the gun barrel and the trigger, and even the bullets lodged inside the gun's chamber, and use that weapon to kill certain police officers, and make it look like Robert Stewart was killing them to cover his tracks as a major criminal and smuggler in New York City. And with Robert Stewart's fingerprints all over the registered smoking gun in his name, and paying off certain people to testify as witnesses who saw him commit those crimes, we can finagle the perfect setup and the perfect frame to have Robert Stewart charged with drug smuggling and mass murder!

"NOW, if we can do this successfully, I as the judge presiding over his case, will make damn sure that Robert Stewart is sentenced to the death penalty for sure! And then that will completely eradicate Robert Stewart from us, FOR GOOD! It would be a much better plan than having Robert Stewart assassinated by a hitman. Because the second attempt on his life using a paid assassin would be too suspicious and certainly may draw heat our way. But to set him up my way, using the law to frame him, and using the justice system to convict him of certain serious charges, will be the perfect method we can utilise to get rid of Robert Stewart finally. Yes. Finally! That, I say, is how we're going to indeed 'eventually' and, after a long time of struggle, at last, be rid of that major obstacle and deadly pain in our arses once and for all!!!"

The three guests who seated before the judge sipping their drinks, nodded their heads at the brilliant plan, and thought to themselves, this idea can work. But they had to come up with the proper detailed aspects of the frame, to ensure that there were no loose ends left behind that could fall apart and bury them alive via any means of exposure, initially, during, and in its aftermath stages, by the failure of succeeding in their elaborate plan to set up Robert Stewart for Major Crimes, which, if successful, would certainly, in their highly opiniated mindsets, result in finally putting every necessary nail and hammering the final nail in Commander Robert Stewart's coffin.

The Priest Vince Archer continued his fears of a possible failure in the execution of their Robert Stewart set up scheme. Priest Vince Archer said, still terrified by the possible fallout of such a plan, and whether they could actually pull it all off. His words were still desperate. His tones became a mixture of nervousness and impatience, as he spoke again, saying the following words, "but can we really succeed in nailing Robert Stewart this way and finally getting rid of him, that pest? I mean, this fucking cop is no ordinary cop. I really have to emphasise that point! This fucking policeman is no ordinary enemy policeman. Every last one of his enemies that had united against him in the past to crush him…had all still failed miserably. Look what happened to my brother recently! My brother called Steven Archer. He is fucking dead in the grave because of that cop Robert Stewart. Are we really sure we can succeed in getting rid of Robert Stewart this way? Are we really sure we can get rid of Robert Stewart any fucking way? I mean, I like your frame idea Judge Lou Larsen. It sounds like a good plan in theory. But can we really put it into practise successfully, without dirtying our hands in the process? And I mean dirtying our hands publicly. Because after executing this plan, can we still successfully remain under the radar? Because based on past history, many people tried to destroy this fucking cop Robert Stewart, but he keeps making comebacks with all his nine lives intact.

"This fucking cop Robert Stewart is no easy kill. But…but… We all have no choice but to go along with it! I even have come up with an idea of how I can help you in your plan to set up Robert Stewart as a drug dealer and mass murderer Judge Lou Larsen. In the confessional as a priest, I hear many tragic stories from many tragic sad cases who come to see me in the confessional. I remember one time long ago a mother was using her six-year-old child daughter as a guinea pig for hypnosis. This mother hypnotised her six-year-old daughter to actually frame her husband she wanted to get rid of, to look guilty of concealing illegal firearms. She would use the child of both hers and her husband's, who her husband would least suspect able to frame him; she would hypnotise that child to plant the guns unsuspectingly inside her husband's car, before she called the police to have him arrested. And when the police searched his car, they found the weapons. Now, this is what she confessed to me inside the confessional. She was a trained hypnotist. But she did not tell me if her plan remained successful in keeping her husband under arrest, or if her husband was actually released or prosecuted. But I found it ingenious that she was able to use the daughter of her husband-the man she hated and wanted to get rid of, to commit a crime against him.

"I am thinking, perhaps we can use a similar strategy against Robert Stewart through our esteemed colleague Psychiatrist Rue Archer present with us today, who operates her psychiatric profession insight the University Hospital in Brooklyn, here in New York. I am sure that Rue Archer comes across many sick children inside the hospital. Rue Archer is a professional psychiatrist. She knows how to manipulate people's emotions and trick them into experiencing complete emotional mental breakdowns. She is a master at planting dark thoughts in people's minds and driving them completely off the rails, even crazy. That's what psychiatrists do best! NOW, as a psychiatrist, she-Rue Archer is also trained in hypnosis. I am sure with her skills she can find the perfect sick child candidate who is admitted in hospital where she works, and arrange for this unsuspecting child patient to be hypnotised without the child's knowledge, to work for us and against Robert Stewart. We can also arrange from one of our wealthy bribing friendly benefactors, who is in fact an experienced drug smuggler in the city, to do us a favour for a price - and bring us certain large quantities of certain bags of heroin and cocaine. We can place these drugs in several bags, giving them to the child who will be targeted by Psychiatrist Rue Archer for hypnosis. And we can, via Rue Archer's hypnoses sessions of the secretly nominated child, have those drugs through this child planted unsuspectingly and unknowingly in Robert Stewart's possession. We can arrange for a scenario where the child's mother or father needs to approach Robert for help. Perhaps we can arrange a burglary at her parents' home. And when the parents utilise

Robert Stewart's services, it will open the door for the child to intertwine herself with Robert Stewart - and unsuspectingly plant the illegal evidence in Robert Stewart's possession, either inside his police station office, or inside his house, or inside his car, or perhaps all three hangouts of his.

"So, if we put our brains together Judge Lou Larsen, I say that indeed the plan to frame Robert Stewart can work. But we need to think out this plan carefully and not make any rash decisions. Because like I said before, every last one of Robert's enemies who united against him to crush his sick arse, ended up failing disastrously and miserably, which resulted in his attackers' imprisonments or deaths or both!"

Judge Lou Larsen nodded his head at his friend, Priest Vince Archer's cautionary speech given to him. And even applauded his suggestion to be considered. Also, Psychiatrist Rue Archer nodded her head and smiled at the priest's brilliant plan of using hypnosis on a sick child inside the hospital she practised psychiatry from to frame Robert Stewart. And even organising a robbery of that child's family home to perfectly open the doors for the child's invitation into Robert Stewart's life. It was a perfect plan she considered. So, Psychiatrist Rue Archer nodded her head at the brilliant scheme and quickly hinted, "I am in! Count me in! I love your scheme with all my black heart, Father Vince Archer. Yes. Oh, yes. Father Vince Archer, the set-up plan of yours against Robert Stewart is certainly one you can count on my full cooperation to put into practise! I will certainly find the perfect child candidate at the University Hospital in Brooklyn to be the perfect frame and patsy to destroy Robert Stewart finally, once and for all! I love the plan. I am certainly one hundred percent in!"

Judge Lou Larsen was equally impressed with his priest friend Vince Archer's salient input into the frame of Robert Stewart. In the judge's mind right now, they were certainly getting a step closer to finagling all the relevant details successfully of how to perfectly set up Robert Stewart for drug dealing and mass murder - and have his conviction stick in court. Prosecuting Brooklyn District Attorney Dave Glick rose from his chair and gave a standing ovation extra-long applause at the plan. And he said ecstatically smiling and laughing, "I love it, I tell you. I fucking love this plan. I believe it can work. I believe that if we can use this sick child to open the doors into Robert Stewart's domain, we can perfectly set him up for a variety of serious offences! And we can get inside his house using this child to locate and steal one of his guns, I am sure he has hidden somewhere inside his house, and use that gun with his fingerprints all over it, to set him up as a murderer on top of having the child plant the drugs in Robert Stewart's possession. After all, how can Commander Robert Stewart possibly suspect an innocent child, no matter how suspicious of a bastard cop he actually is?

"We can also pay off witnesses to finger Robert Stewart in the murders and the drug deals. And I would be assigned as the prosecuting district attorney in the case against Robert Stewart. And with me prosecuting the case and with you Judge Lou Larsen presiding as the ultimate verdict decision-maker and absolute ruling instigator in the sentencing in the case against Robert Stewart, we will both succeed. We should both succeed in finally crucifying Commander Robert Stewart and getting him out of our lives for good, using the law instead of using outside-of-the-law tactics which have failed in the past. But if we can manipulate the justice system to work against Robert Stewart as we have manipulated the justice system to fix cases and verdict decisions in our favour in the past, I say that Robert Stewart can finally be dealt with successfully in this measure!"

CHAPTER 5

Robert Stewart had a death stare in his eyes as he listened, watched, recorded and studied the continuous evil conversations of the four targets he was dying right now to have each of them hanged by their necks brutally and viciously. And now Robert Stewart and his police surveillance team posted aside him inside the law-enforcement surveillance vehicle, would listen to the mentally sick and twisted Priest Vince Archer continue his insane words at this time, stealing the limelight before his partners in crime, as they were all situated inside the judge's chambers. The hideous diseased lunatic Priest Vince Archer was 'all for' the monstrous idea but equally shared his mixed feelings of fear at the sordid plan, all the same, being put in motion rather concurrently!

All in all, even though the corrupt priest eldest brother of Elliot Archer, named Vince Archer, was all in favour of the heinously murderous plan to set up and frame Robert for being an illegal drug smuggler and mass murderer, he still could not help his psychotic brain's thought patterns fluctuating back and forth at this moment, from overjoy in the idea, to being a killjoy wet blanket party pooper to the irrational scheme. His negative thought patterns suddenly took over his mindset unhelped, as he once again interrupted the discussions through his negative thinking, and shouted in a sudden flurry of terrified thought patterns that took over his conscious mind, as the true candidate of obsessive-compulsive disorder his friend Psychiatrist Rue Archer failed to diagnose, and simply ignored and dismissed altogether prejudicially in his case as his friend, when the corrupt Priest Vince Archer raised his voice in horrified thoughts, saying before his three lunatic companions in judicial crimes, "Again, I cannot help my negative thinking. WHAT IF SOMETHING GOES WRONG? What if something goes fucking wrong in this sick plan of ours? What if we fail? What if we don't succeed? I still cannot forget past history. Can't you all remember you sick lunatics present with me here this evening inside these chambers? Can't you remember what happened to all those people who tried to play games with Robert Stewart? Can you not remember what happened to those fucking idiots who tried Robert Stewart in the past, both recent and distant? **So many of them fucking died!!! So many of them lost their fucking lives!** Everyone who united against

Robert Stewart to bring him down and destroy him and kill him have failed! So, you think that we can finally succeed in this insane plan of ours, which I think is brilliant, but still, nothing in this world is foolproof, especially when it entails going against a menacing, cleverly dangerous cop such as Commander Robert Stewart.

"I mean, let me say again and again and fucking repeat again - what if we fail? What happens to us if we are not victorious? Can we actually pull this off and fool the entire justice system by framing Robert Stewart for drug smuggling and fucking mass murder? Is it really possible to do all this and keep our hands clean in the process, undetected as the ones responsible for sending Robert Stewart to prison, and possibly to the fucking gas chamber? HUH! Can we actually work this plan successfully without Robert Stewart suspecting anything - and catch him by surprise before he can do anything to extricate himself out of his own sealed fate by our hands? And if we do pull it off, can we actually get away with it permanently, whilst continuing our hypocritical facades before the world as harmless beings? Can we continue our facades and keep the masks plastered on our two-faced exteriors before the public, and conceal that we are in fact masterminds trying to play Robert Stewart's chessboard game, and this time, flipping the game over and making Robert Stewart follow our game with our rules and our instructions, to seal his fate into a coffin once and for all? I mean, how do we know that we are going to have the last laugh? How do we know that Robert Stewart is not going to have the last laugh? How do we know that Robert Stewart is not going to become privy to our grand scheme, even before we put all the pieces of the puzzle into practical motion? How do we know that Robert Stewart is not sensing what we are doing as we speak? I mean, this fucking cop Robert Stewart must be a mind reader or something.

"Look, look, look at everything that has happened... Look at what he did to Steven Archer and his so-called great plan to clip him? Robert Stewart stopped my brother cold, right along with all those other co-conspirator doctors and nurses and psychologists dead in their tracks! Robert Stewart is not to be toyed with! That fact has been proven time and time again! Anyone who tests Robert Stewart ends up in a very deadly position! In simple terms, they all become extinct!!! They are now all in the ground dead because of Robert Stewart. How do we know that Robert Stewart is not sensing what we are doing right now? How do we know that Robert Stewart is not looming over our heads, reminiscent to some dark cloud, ready to blow us away into the ground dead as my brother, as my younger brother Steven Archer ended up? And let us not forget, he ended up that way by the hands of Robert Stewart. And why did Robert Stewart kill him? Because my younger brother Steven Archer tried to play with Robert Stewart and ended up dead as a consequence for trying to play with him. Are we conveniently forgetting that? Here we are trying to play with Robert Stewart as well. It is as if we are also suicidal - and trying to sign our own death warrants the same way as my younger brother Steven Archer signed his death warrant recently, by trying to challenge our archenemy rival, Commander Robert Stewart.

"LOOK. I know we have our plans. We have plotted and schemed to destroy Robert Stewart! But…but…but… How do we know that Robert Stewart is not some sort of ghost hiding somewhere inside this judge's chambers listening to us? How do we know we're going to pull off what we're plotting and scheming to pull off against him successfully? I cannot stop the fears inside my mind growing, gnawing at me. All of a sudden, I'm grinding my teeth. I'm gnashing my teeth, as if I'm being attacked by that fiendish Robert Stewart's spirit as we speak. Because all his enemies in the past had great plans and great schemes to bring Robert Stewart to his knees. And the one fundamental error they made was they all underestimated him, at the same time as he was acting as a silent shadow over them, studying their plans, and understanding what they were up to like some sadistic evil dark silent ghost planted surreptitiously around them.

"Everybody else in the past thought they had a great plan against Robert Stewart. But Robert Stewart all the while was silently studying their weaknesses - and using those weaknesses against them, to bring them all down! **And many of them are dead in the ground.** How do we know that as we brag and plot and scheme, Robert Stewart is not somehow invisibly surrounding us, listening to us, and plotting our own downfalls to take place, before we even can draft the final stage of our supposed masterful plan to destroy him? Here we are mocking Robert Stewart, but where is Robert Stewart right now? Where is that invisible ghost named Commander Robert Stewart positioned? How do we know Robert Stewart has not assumed the role of spiritual assassin planted inside this room, listening to us, waiting to invade our private space and kill us, after we have exposed ourselves, the same way he killed my brother, Psychiatrist Steven Archer! Robert Stewart is a master fighter, a brilliant mental strategist, who has plotted, schemed and planned the demises of a great many men and women in the past. We cannot forget that! Robert Stewart is an earthquake, a thunderstorm, wreaking constant havoc in our lives! **He is a fucking natural disaster wrapped in an enigma of silence!** He plots the downfalls of criminals like us in the dark, in the quiet and then moves against us faster than lightning.

"Here we are thinking that Robert Stewart is some sort of sitting duck lamb. But what Robert Stewart really is, is a dangerous wolf waiting to attack his prey, meaning us, with his very sharp teeth, and with his weapons of war: his guns, his bullets, his fucking sword and his all-powerful frigging police badge of honour! Robert Stewart let's people think they are winning, when all the while he is scheming his delicious terror of destruction against all those, who think they will get away with destroying him. And when he strikes against criminals like us, we can forget about begging and asking for mercy. Because Robert Stewart will give no mercy to us! He will simply attack us and throw the book at us. He will either cuff our hands and have us sentenced to prison for the rest of our lives, or he will most certainly kill us right then and there on the spot with his guns and bullets! This man Robert Stewart is a true chess master. He waits, he plots, he plans and he schemes against all his targets silently, without any of us getting wind of what he is up to. I have a feeling, a sick gnawing feeling that Robert Stewart is surrounding us right now, listening to us, waiting for us to expose ourselves fully, before he moves in for the kill, just as he moved in to terrorise and finally killed my brother, Psychiatrist Steven Archer! It's like, where are you, Robert Stewart? Where are you hidden inside this room Robert Stewart? You deadly, deadly beast. You deadly, deadly silent ghost, plotting our destructions, whilst all the while waiting for us to reveal our hands and celebrate our plans to end you prematurely… Yes. We celebrate prematurely. But it is Robert Stewart who is smiling and laughing at us, as he is silently and invisibly gathering all the evidence against us, to slaughter us like lambs, that sick and twisted deadly wolf Commander Robert Stewart surely is! Yes, Robert Stewart. I know how you operate. You let us think we have the advantage and then you strike at us when we never see you coming!

"I don't know about the rest of you, but I feel that man's presence around us. I feel his invisible power, the fire inside him; the volcanic deadly earthquake that is just silently waiting to unleash against us in deadly tornadoes when we least expect it. I know he is hiding someplace around us, smiling and laughing, waiting to strike and attack us and take us all by surprise, without us knowing that we're going to be hit by his all-consuming powers and lunatic wrathful vengeance at any moment now, unsuspectingly to us anyway!

"You think Robert Stewart is a victim? Here we are plotting his downfall as if Robert Stewart is a victim. The truth is, Robert Stewart is not able to be a victim! Robert Stewart is certainly no victim. He is a cold-hearted malicious executioner of criminals such as us! Robert Stewart has succeeded against every enemy he has come across in the past. And here we are thinking that we're going to be the ones finally able to pull off his destruction? Who the fuck do we think we are kidding? Robert Stewart came up against the best. Robert Stewart had beaten long odds in his life. Robert Stewart had beaten savage monsters in the past, and here we are thinking we're going to beat him? How fucking absurd! How do we know that Robert Stewart is not setting us up for the very death sentence we are in fact planning for him? How do we know Robert Stewart is not going to enter these chambers very shortly and execute each and every one of us, for our sick plans against him? How the fuck do we know anything? Are we blind? Are we deaf? Are we fucking stupid? How fucking ignorant are we? To ignore past history of how that cold-blooded executioner Robert Stewart dealt with the most monstrous antagonistic human scum driven against him! Here we are plotting Robert Stewart's destruction, whilst ignoring the fact that Robert Stewart single-handedly engineered the destruction of the most vicious monsters that ever walked the streets of our society. We think we're going to succeed in our fucking devious plan to frame and imprison Robert Stewart for drugs and mass murder?

"There were armies of enemies of Robert Stewart in the past who engineered great plans to destroy him and they all fucking failed. But we think...we are here thinking delusional ideas that we are going to succeed with our sick plan to imprison that monster demon threatening enemy wolf with sharp teeth called Robert Stewart? Many people in this world are soft and predictable. But Robert Stewart is a hard bastard. He is completely unpredictable. And we are being careless right now in our plans, planning his destruction whilst ignoring the true ingenious capabilities and destructive powers of this man, our number one enemy, called Robert Stewart. We can plan to destroy harmless people, weak people, cowards. But we are planning to destroy a man who is in fact a harmful, strong, resilient and courageous cop called, Commander Robert Stewart! This is a feat beyond everybody else's capabilities, PERIOD! And we think we can engineer some diabolical plan to get rid of him, when everybody else in the past who were pure evil fucking sadistic mass murdering monsters, failed to destroy this one cop Robert Stewart. Are we truly deaf, dumb, blind and fucking stupid idiots to ignore such facts, to ignore past history and the incredibly unmatched capabilities of this one extraordinary cop Robert Stewart?

"Here we are planning his downfall, when in truth, what we do not know is that Robert Stewart is most likely playing us for suckers. He is plotting and scheming like a ghost, an invisible ghost in the darkness, our murders as we speak. This fucking cop is going to end up destroying all of us, I can feel it in my very dark soul! Robert Stewart is the ultimate gamesman. What he is doing right now with his silence is playing mind games with us. He is giving us exactly what we want right now. Freedom of thought, freedom of speech and freedom of conspired criminal actions. He is waiting all the while for us to 'fully' incriminate ourselves, so he can then make his final move and come after us with more than just the full weight of the law behind him. But he plans to come after us with murderous intents to remove our sick existences from this world completely, before we even can dream of removing him from our lives! That is Robert Stewart! That is how this fucking sick sadistic brilliant cop Robert Stewart operates. He operates in the shadows. He is a true mastermind.

"Here we are thinking we are silently getting away with our schemes and illegal actions, but it is really Robert Stewart who is engineering our deaths invisibly, in a cold-and-calculated, brilliantly masterful genius-like exercise! Robert Stewart is not only a genius at his artistic craft of law enforcement, but he is truly dangerous. He is truly brilliant at destroying his targets - and that is what truly makes him **'unforgettable',** especially in my mind's estimation right now. I truly am feeling overwhelming fear inside of me by Robert's all-consuming presence, his invisible threatening presence surrounding us. I don't know, but I'm just feeling his invisible aura around us, around all of us! He is silently waiting for us to completely expose ourselves, before he moves in to blow us away to kingdom come! Here we are wearing titles as Priest, Judge, District Attorney, Psychiatrist. Hiding behind masks in a hypocritical society of fools, liars, thieves, murderers, rapists and all forms of scum, but we are pretentious scumbags ourselves, only disguised with reputable and respectable titles. But you want to know who is the cleverest at wearing disguises and hiding his true abilities and presence from his prey? It is Robert Stewart! It is Commander Robert Stewart! Robert Stewart is the true master of disguise! Robert Stewart is the true mover and shaker and instigator of agonies and torments against dirtbags like us!

"Robert Stewart remains silent. Robert Stewart maintains his mask of discreteness and his facade of ignorance against us and our sick plans. And then…then…then…fucking then… **BOOM!** Yes. Fucking boom! He looms at us like an invisible spiritual assassin, a ghost, a horror story told to children by their parents!

"Let me snap all of you people present inside this room out of your delusional states, and back to reality. Robert Stewart is an assassin. Robert Stewart is a master assassin. Compared to him, we are inexperienced fucking amateurs. Robert Stewart is letting us think we're going to destroy him and get away with it, before he will finally surface from out of nowhere and change the script on our destinies, leaving us pissing and shitting our pants from the shock and fear of his wrath, when he finally makes his move to strike at us, ferociously, with his deadly malicious powers of elimination against creeps and scumbags like us present inside this judge's chambers. But surely, he doesn't care about our pretentious fancy titles. He doesn't care about the masks we wear, pretending to be perfect individuals in society. With one stare at close-range and from a distance in our direction, Robert Stewart will unmask our facades and see through the hypocritical operations we disguise ourselves in front of the world. And he will truly unravel the sick and twisted individuals we are before the whole world, as justification for his ambush, his deadly ambush and elimination of our lives. And the spilling of our blood before the world, that will become his audience. The world is not our audience. The world is his audience when he executes us!

"So, everybody inside this room, PAY ATTENTION. This is not some fictitious story! This is cold-hearted fucking reality! This is the sick reality we face by this venomous enemy of ours called Commander Robert Stewart! Yes. We can fool the entire world of suckers with our lies, deceitfully hypocritical fancy titles and phoney masks we wear every day of our lives before the people we come across. But we cannot fool Robert Stewart. You think we are playing a game against society and against Robert Stewart? No, my esteemed colleagues. We are not playing a game, especially against Robert Stewart. **Because if truth be told, Robert Stewart is the game.** Robert Stewart has flipped the script and taken over the rule book of every game out there, including and especially ours! He flips the board of our games and replaces it with his chessboard. And his chess game! And then he forces us to play with rules that we do not know or have been educated in instruction manuals of such combat and retaliation. So, when we are forced to play Robert Stewart's game with his rules and hidden secret instructions that only he masters, that's why us criminals always lose against him!

"Here we are planning to make a masterful move against Robert Stewart. But the so-called clever people gathered inside this room right now, are really not that clever. If truth be known, we are being very reckless and very stupid in regards to Robert Stewart!!! Because what we are simply ignoring, the horrible insidious fearful truth what we are ignoring, is that Robert Stewart silently and invisibly has already predicted each and every one of our moves in advance, before we have even planned such moves against him. That is what we have ignored. That is the Horror Story that we simply did not know all along. Robert Stewart has predicted all our moves right to the minutest detail, before we have written the final draft of whatever sick plans we have concocted in our sick minds against society and against him, Robert Stewart himself!

"Robert Stewart is laughing at our weaknesses; at the same time as we have conveniently but foolishly ignored his extraordinary strengths that he will utilise against us in the final checkmate move he renders in this game of his, with his rules he will force us to play, when he finally confronts us and brings us down to the very hell we have ignored the existence of, since the beginning of our wretched lives in this world! Robert Stewart is a ghost. Robert Stewart is an invisible haunting enemy. He is the one enemy in this world that we truly have no defences against. He is truly the only enemy in this world that we cannot compete against! How the fuck are we ignoring that painful truth as we sit here thinking and concocting plans of his destruction? Because as we are making our plans, whilst laughing at Robert Stewart, Robert Stewart has already defeated us in his own invisible horrendously victorious doomsday operation he has in the reckoning for each and every one of us. As he sits there invisibly watching us without our knowledge, Robert Stewart relishes allowing his enemies to underestimate him, until he finally confronts us and forces us to die in the shame of embarrassment, humiliation, degradation and despair at our ignorance, that he was playing us all along, whilst using trickery and manipulation tactics to make us think that we were playing him. And we are only going to realise that fact after he confronts us and forces us to drown in our own blood he spills from our bodies in the final confrontation he has orchestrated against us, to come to fruition shortly!

"Robert Stewart beats us crooked people just through his fearful knowledge he has, by stopping our defences, whilst at the same time penetrating through our hypocritical masks. Robert Stewart is just playing a waiting game. But what we have to realise, is that he is fooling us brilliantly, cleverly, masterfully and undeniably! And that is Robert Stewart's poetic justice against us! That is Robert Stewart's ultimate revenge against dirtbags like us! In truth, we are the pawns on Robert Stewart's chessboard game. He is playing us like fools! It is Robert Stewart running the show, nobody else. We are not masterminds in any scheme. It is Robert Stewart who is the true mastermind in the grand scheme of things! And Robert Stewart's INVISIBILITY right now is serving his purpose in the delicious revenge he has planned against us all.

"We are not planning anything successfully. It is Robert Stewart who is planning our downfalls successfully, PERIOD! Robert Stewart is hiding somewhere laughing at us right now. He is truly playing us for the very fools we are!!! Robert Stewart's silence is strategy, his secret deadly weapon. His hidden knowledge against us is his strength. And with all that knowledge and strategy produces the ultimate power that Robert Stewart exudes to finally destroy us, before we are able to exit this building this evening! So, friends and colleagues, mark my words: **we are all dead**

before we exit these chambers this evening. We are not going to ever be able to enter our homes alive ever again! Robert Stewart has already killed us! And that truth is what we haven't even realised yet. But we will shortly! Because like I said, Robert Stewart has been playing us all along. And we have just simply ignored it, by playing into his hands and exposing ourselves as sitting ducks to his wrathful presence and poetic justice he will shortly unleash against all of us, when he and his armies of police enter this judge's chambers and shoot to kill, yes, he will give the order to open fire and shoot-to-kill each and every one of us. Robert Stewart is making us think that we are winning. But let me repeat, Robert Stewart is playing us. He is simply using mathematical calculations and scientific strategies to engineer our death sentences! Robert Stewart is just sitting back and letting us relish in our arrogance and our stupid ignorance. He is targeting us as a silent executioner and he is the one truly setting us up and framing us for death and destruction, not the other way around.

"Robert Stewart is listening to us. Robert Stewart is watching us. Robert Stewart wants us to become careless and clumsy via our mediocre and average at best, half-cocked overconfidence. You think we have plans to set up Robert Stewart for destruction? No, my dishonourable friends and disgustingly immoral colleagues. It is the other way around. Robert Stewart has just dug up our graves, and he is waiting for us to give him all the ammunition he needs, before he throws us inside and buries us into the dirt alive.

"We were never the predators. But Robert Stewart was always the hunter, with the innate uncanny superpowers of perception skills and putting two-and-two together! You think we can hide things from Robert Stewart? We cannot hide anything from Robert Stewart. Robert Stewart is a force of nature. Robert Stewart has supernatural powers. He has unexplainable gifts and remarkable abilities to read people's emotions and read people's thoughts, even from a terrific distance! Robert Stewart always knows who his enemies are and what they are plotting against, not only the community, but also against him. He knows who is about to cross him even before those people know they are planning to cross him! Robert Stewart knows every dirty trick in the book. Even the devil in hell fears him and stays away from him! The devil fears his supernatural perceptive powers! Robert Stewart knows every dirty dark secret that everyone is trying to hide from him. He has the unique gifted ability to expose people's hidden skeletons that no other person alive has the ability to accomplish. No one can keep a secret from Robert Stewart. No one can keep their dirty dark schemes and hideously wicked and evil plans from him. Robert Stewart always uncovers the uncoverable! Robert always unmasks the facades of all manipulators who have been able to fool the rest of the world. Robert Stewart sees through deception to the envy of every fraud and amateur psychiatrist that exists in this world!

"Look. We have to understand here who we are dealing with. We have to think twice, three times, ten fucking times…one hundred and one thousand times, before trying to plot any moves behind Robert Stewart's back. Because believe me, Robert Stewart will know everything that we are doing before we even know the precise details of what the hell we are on about and what the fuck we are planning behind Commander Robert Stewart's back! Robert Stewart is an uncanny mind-reader. Robert Stewart is a notorious and infamous mask destroyer. He can spot a hypocrite from another country. He can spot a crime before all the details of that crime are carefully planned. Robert Stewart is a walking doomsday machine.

He is the evil sadistic magician that forces us to sleep with two eyes open at night, wondering if it is us he is going to target next. He is the Walking Karma in our lives, that forces us to live in horrified terror of what knowledge he has amassed against us and our sinful crimes. How can we be in peace thinking that we can defeat such an invisible master and deviously secretive walking terror as that? I know that right now through the ill feelings that I have going on inside me, that I will never be able to sleep again.

"I know Robert Stewart is on to me. I know that Robert Stewart is on to us. THAT FUCKING COP ROBERT STEWART KNOWS EVERYTHING!!! He knows that we are gunning for him right now. He knows that I, Father Vince Archer has arrived here today at this judge's chambers, with two briefcases each stuffed with $500,000, to pay to each of you American-born friends of mine, District Attorney Dave Glick and Judge Lou Larsen, such exorbitant monies to ensure that you fix my brother Elliot Archer's upcoming court case trial, to result in his acquittal in its aftermath. And Robert Stewart also knows all the wretchedly wicked plans we have against him, to frame him for very serious Major Crimes, that would result in his arrest and his prosecution by District Attorney Dave Glick, and his guilty verdict and harsh sentencing to be handed down to him by Judge Lou Larsen! Robert Stewart knows everything! And because he knows, that means that we are all finished! We really have no option but to kill ourselves right now. Because any second now, Robert Stewart is going to enter the doors of this judge's chambers to do us all in. We have to ask ourselves a question? Do we want Robert Stewart to have that final victory against us and to humiliate us inside his jail cell, or do we want to take the easy way out and simply make sure that once he enters this judge's chambers, he is only left to witness our dead corpses? We have to decide quickly! I say let us not let Robert Stewart take us alive!" Insisted Priest Vince Archer to his three friends of mutually diabolically shady characters present with him inside the meeting place they attended together that night.

CHAPTER 6

In Robert Stewart's mind that evening, the moment had arrived. Robert Stewart penetrated through the masks worn by the four targets called District Attorney Dave Glick, Judge Lou Larsen, Priest Vince Archer and Psychiatrist Rue Archer. Robert Stewart exposed the insidious hypocrisy and unravelled their three-phase plan of death and destruction. And now the truth of it all was going to detonate against them as powerfully as truckloads of atomic and nuclear bombs all combined; to blow up their entire worlds into the abyss they planned unsuccessfully for so many others in society, by using or abusing the powers of the justice system as their money-making manipulative scam, permanently. But failed on that score of permanence.

Robert Stewart had gathered all the beautiful evidence he needed to send them packing their bags into the Next World, South of their feet!

And now as their doomsday reckoning had arrived, District Attorney Dave Glick, Judge Lou Larsen, Priest Vince Archer and Psychiatrist Rue Archer had only realised when it was all too late, that the man called Robert Stewart they each plotted to destroy, was in fact the one true destroyer and killer of disguises and illusions, such as the masks those four felonious fiends had worn throughout their lives and careers, hiding their fraud and incompetence behind fancy titles, whilst at the same time, using the very weak and flimsy justice system as their cover, to get away with their crimes in a united front, as scam operators within the otherwise impenetrable walls of the judicial system.

Now they were each faced with their spiritual assassin, their justice-serving executioner named Robert Stewart. Robert Stewart not only shattered their illusions that they had utilised to control, to twist words and manipulate the justice system to no end, but he also stripped them of their fake confidence and broke their egos at the same time, as he unleashed his poetic justice to revoke not only their titles, but their freedoms permanently!

Now the four dreadful targets unanimously faced their own demises and imprisonments. Crazy District Attorney Dave Glick, insane Judge Lou Larsen, corrupt Priest Vince Archer and insidious Psychiatrist Rue Archer were forced to ask themselves one question: was I really that clever? The answer was an obvious 'no'. Because they were unable to fool the one person they could never fool, and that was Commander Robert Stewart. So now they were faced with a predicament of dread being thrown their way from all directions. They were experiencing no simple demotion. But they were facing complete dismissal of their fancy titles and shame and embarrassment by the one cop they plotted to destroy; that one master cop called Robert Stewart had brilliantly outsmarted them, outwitted them and outmanoeuvred them without them knowing the truth until it was all too late. And it was that truth that Robert was playing them and not the other way around, that struck them the hardest emotionally, physically and spiritually to complete breaking point they experienced at this present time.

Their scams of using and abusing the justice system for years had finally come to the surface, was exposed to the entire world and was ended once and for all in their miserable defeats.

And they sorely considered Robert Stewart the mark of a true assassin. Because when he entered the judge's chambers to arrest all of them, the guilt and shame his targets felt, forced them to each kill themselves before they could be dragged into the abyss, South of their feet, by first being arrested as a prelude to that destined demise waiting for them. Mad crazy District Attorney Dave Glick, certifiably insane Judge Lou Larsen, wickedly corrupt Priest Vince Archer and the viciously detestable Psychiatrist Rue Archer had placed Cyanide pills (also known as suicide pills), in the palms of their right hands, once Priest Vince Archer warned them that they were sitting ducks to Robert Stewart earlier that evening inside the judge's chambers. It was the Priest Vince Archer who always carried Cyanide pills with him after his brother's recent passing. He was haunted by his brother's death just days before at the hands of Robert Stewart. So paranoia and fear that he may face the same judgement and destruction by the commander's hands, had him well-equipped and well-prepared in advance, to escape the humiliation of prison, by taking his own life if he was faced with a precarious situation of Robert Stewart's surprising looming presence appearing before him, at a time that warranted poetic justice to be delivered against him.

Just as they heard the police footsteps outside the judge's chambers, and only seconds before the police entered the office room, the priest handed suicide pills comprising of Cyanide poisoning to each of his fake and phoney friends and colleagues situated inside the judge's chambers, as an easy outlet and an easier escape, to prevent prosecution and imprisonment for their crimes, by swallowing the poisons only moments before the police, led by Robert Stewart, stormed the doors of the judge's chambers, to do them justice through the firm arm of the justice system, against those four targets who had otherwise plotted and schemed to wreck and destroy for years, that very judicial system institution, notably through the heinous actions of the judge and the district attorney in question.

Robert Stewart wanted to prosecute them 'all' with that very same justice system they each mocked, cheated and scammed throughout their criminal careers as district attorney, judge, priest and psychiatrist. Dave Glick was the Assistant District Attorney previously in Manhattan, then recently elected blindly as the official District Attorney, serving in that part of New York, as was Lou Larsen a judge in that borough, before transferring themselves to Brooklyn much recently, to unleash the same chaos and havoc and corruption and destruction, within the Brooklyn Judicial System as they had for years in the Manhattan Borough of New York City and New York State.

But now their chaos and corruption had come to an end. And in themselves, they took the easy way out by committing suicide with the swallowing of Cyanide pills before the police could arrest them.

Robert Stewart and his army of police reinforcements entering the judge's chambers, had witnessed the four deaths of the targeted individuals, now their corpses lying motionless on to the mixture of rug and parquetry floors of the deceased judge's domain. And that finally ended the judicial system corruption workings of District Attorney Dave Glick, Judge Lou Larsen, with the collaboration of Priest Vince Archer and Psychiatrist Rue Archer!

CHAPTER 7

Robert Stewart was certainly considered a man with nine lives. And bad news travelled fast. Once Elliot Archer quickly received word that evening that his oldest brother Vince Archer and his collaborators in the crime and scam to have him released from his incarceration, such as the judge and the district attorney's failed attempts, which also cost them their lives, Elliot Archer now stood inside his jail cell in utter shock and disbelief at the poetic brilliance of Robert Stewart's masterminded victory yet again, to thwart their attempts, not only outwitting him, Elliot Archer in particular, but at the same time, sabotaging what could have been a very clean plot to a very twisted plan, that may have worked precisely in Elliot Archer's favour, had his priest brother, the judge and the district attorney, specifically and notably, not lost their lives. But now that the instrumental key figures that could have assisted him in his release and acquittal in his upcoming trial were dead, Elliot Archer knew there was no hope for his escape from jail. And in the upcoming trial, not only was he going to be found guilty without District Attorney Dave

Glick and Judge Lou Larsen fixing his trial and verdict outcome to 'not guilty', but Elliot Archer knew that his sentencing would result in his complete destruction. And truly the failure of all his further attempts to try to safeguard his freedom, PERIOD!

Again, Elliot Archer was in sheer disbelief. That cunning sonofabitch Robert Stewart won again. He won again and again and again. And as Elliot Archer stood inside his jail cell clasping his hands around the steel bars, he shook his head from side to side in dismay and bewilderment at Robert Stewart's victory against him, yet again. And he thought to himself the following words buzzing around in his head ferociously and unhelped in the aftermath of the failed deed of his escape from lockup: ah, look at you. Look at you Robert Stewart. You are still breathing, living and breathing our further attempts to have you gone! And in the process, you killed my second brother, my eldest brother, Priest Vince Archer. You are truly Robert Stewart, a walking nightmare, a curse, a walking curse. How is it possible that you have defeated us this time, yet again? How is it possible that we have lost so much because of your blasphemous existence? Ah Robert Stewart. You truly are an enigma. You truly are a mysterious dark cloud hanging over all our heads. You have ruined me this evening Robert Stewart. You have truly ruined me. You know what I am Robert Stewart? You know what I really am? I'm a fucking dead man because of you Robert Stewart! You hear me, Robert Stewart? You have just killed me at the same time that you caused my brother Vince Archer's death. You killed my brother Psychiatrist Steven Archer and now you resulted in the death of my esteemed priestly oldest brother Vince Archer. You have destroyed me, Robert Stewart. Now there is no escape from your clutches. Now there is no hope that I can escape what you have done to me. I am fucked Robert Stewart. I am totally screwed because of you. My best laid plans are all dead in the water. I am fucked Robert Stewart. I am literally fucked. You have destroyed me single-handedly my enemy Robert Stewart.

And as I stand here inside this jail cell in your horrible custody confined like an animal, I realise I have no hope anymore left in my situation. You defeated me, Robert Stewart. You defeated me yet again. How? How did you do it? Perhaps I was never even a crumb of the great cop you always were. But still, I cannot believe I lost so badly. I cannot believe that everyone who was willing to help me is now dead. And my situation as a result of those deaths, those precious deaths of all those precious people close to me, means that I am doomed to destruction and despair. I am completely finished right now. You hear me, Robert Stewart? You have finished me. I'm gone! I am gone! You have destroyed me this evening Robert Stewart. You have totally wiped me out for good. And I have no escape. There is no one left in this cruel, cold world of ours who is going to help me. There are no scams to concoct any further. No more escape attempts. No one is going to help me and risk the exposure of my departure from jail out of your clutches, your horrible, confined custody. I have lost because of you Robert Stewart. And damn it all to hell, you have won Robert Stewart. You have beat me, Robert Stewart. You have completely fucked me up Robert Stewart. I am fucked Robert Stewart because of you Commander Robert Stewart. You have completely stuffed me up too. I'm totally fucked! What the hell am I gonna do now?

There is nothing left for me to do except one course of action that I must take to escape this. It will be a desperate action. But it is a necessary action. I cannot be sentenced to life imprisonment because of you Robert Stewart. You have forced me to take the same drastic but necessary actions as my priestly brother and his friends took this evening. That's the easiest, the only escape for me. Just one course of action that remains in my chaotically dire situation. Just one recourse I have left in me. And that is to end it all here and right now. Because I will not let you take me to prison Robert Stewart. I will not let you send me to maximum-security prison for the rest of my life. I will not give you the ultimate satisfaction Robert Stewart, of watching me squirm in maximum-security prison for the rest of my days. I must do what my brother Vince Archer did, just to escape your spiderweb trap that you have entangled all of us with tonight. That you have entrapped ME by!

You are a walking curse Robert Stewart. You are a walking nightmare Robert Stewart. And I must emphasise that over and over and over again, until my life is no longer amongst the living for you to torment and torture any further. As much as it pains me to admit it, I have to admit the truth that you Robert Stewart, are simply unbeatable! Not only are you clever, you're a fucking unsung heroic genius. You are too smart for all of us! You beat us again, Commander Robert Stewart. You fucking beat us at our own manipulative game. I have no recourse but to end things right now in the only fashion that remains, so that I can finally escape the bitter and vicious wrath of you Commander Robert Stewart. And I must escape you once and for all by that final action left in me that I must take, that is necessary for me to take, to prevent you from having me locked up for the rest of my days! I cannot let you have the ultimate victory of embarrassing me and humiliating me to a sentence of life behind bars. I must use the death of my wonderful priestly brother Vince Archer as an example, as a textbook example of how to break loose and hightail it all from your vengeance Robert Stewart.

I must use my brother Vince Archer's teachings and guidance of how to escape the domineering control and ruthless retribution of that one damn cop, who is a walking catastrophe. And that predator's horrific name is, Commander Robert Stewart! I have no choice, but to exercise my freewill and my right to end things the way I want things to be ended! You will not take me alive Robert Stewart. You will not destroy the rest of my life Robert Stewart. Because I will remove my existence from this world my way, not your way Robert Stewart.

You have already defeated me countless times, Commander. But I will not allow you to outshine me and ridicule me inside the hellhole you have in store for me! No, Commander Robert Stewart. I cannot allow your wretched disastrous plans of complete human degradation against me to succeed as well. I must escape your hold, your wicked clutches in the only way that is available to me to escape you. And that is death itself!

All our plans to make you be gone had failed Robert Stewart. We planned your death; we planned to have you set up and framed as a vicious criminal roaming the streets of New York. We planned your funeral too damn soon. Because all our plans backfired! We had the flowers to lay on your gravestone and gravesite all ready. We had the instruction manual drafted of how we were going to destroy your reputation Robert Stewart and frame you as a sick maniac. We had everything prepared, including having your nameplate inscribed with your name and rank title inside-and-outside your police station office doors removed, literally burnt off with fire. We had your final farewell all lined up, much like a comical parade. We spent all that time working out your downfall and yet here you are Robert Stewart, intercepting all our sick plans against you, and throwing those plans in the trash, at the same time as you tossed our lives away into the garbage bin as garbage disposal, of all our dead corpses. After all that effort to try to mastermind your downfall and destruction, here you are Robert Stewart, still fucking breathing. Still fucking alive. You had dismantled all our predictions and estimates behind closed doors that you were a certified dead man. You truly outshone all of us Robert Stewart. Yes. You certainly did. You truly outshined us.

Robert Stewart…you were not supposed to be alive today. You were not supposed to be in the position to go to work tomorrow. You are supposed to be doomed! We had invested so much time and energy to disrupt your usual narrative of going to work every day and arresting the bad people. Your entire existence had defied our obituary rehearsal we had in the works for you Robert Stewart. Your entire existence has proven to be a glitch in all our plans. We wanted your ending, Robert Stewart!!! But instead, you delivered a series of continuous sequels, chilling comebacks of your games of cat and mouse and hunter and hunted.

And in truth, you rewrote the whole script we had in store for you. We were never hunting you; you were always hunting us from the beginning of this horrible story of cop versus the bad guy. You cheated death Robert Stewart. And in so doing that one death-defying deed, time and time again, you simply went against our rules and expectations of constructing the beautiful death sentence we had in mind for you! You fucked up our entire timelines. Because not only did we design and create the precise details of your ruin, fall and ultimate death, we also engineered the entire collapse of your way of doing things down at police headquarters. We wanted to put a complete stop to how you were running investigations successfully against criminals such as us.

I mean, fuck your style of policing Robert Stewart. Fuck your success stories of putting us criminals behind bars. We wanted to end your victorious streak against all of us bad people, like a puff of smoke! And we also wanted to end you hard!

But no Robert Stewart. You had to keep doing things your way, didn't you Commander Robert Stewart. You always have to keep winning against us evildoers, don't you Commander. You always have to get your fucking way and outshine our attempts to fuck you over. You always have to win. And we always have to lose, as the nutjob fuckwit bad guy lunatics that you keep proving we are.

To tell you the truth Robert Stewart, I am sick of you finagling the rulebook to always serve in your favour against ugly shits like me. I am sick of coming last in my efforts to outsmart you. I can't take it anymore. I can't take it anymore. I can't take it anymore. You see Robert Stewart, you have truly turned me into a nutcase. I'm even repeating my words because of you, you sick sadistic, evil, mad maniacal genius. I'm really repeating myself here. You have completely driven me crazy. You have completely driven me over the edge Robert Stewart. I just can't take losing anymore. I just can't take losing anymore. I just can't take losing anymore. And in order to escape my losses and your wins, I will do what my beautiful pure-hearted priest brother Vince Archer did to escape your evil wicked clutches, Commander Robert Stewart. And that is, I will terminate my existence from this world just to escape you, Commander Robert Stewart!

Me-myself-and-I, the district attorney, the judge, my priest brother and our psychiatrist colleague, had our parts to play in your downfall Robert Stewart. But it all fell through. We created the script of your downfall, narrated the removal of you from your job, and crafted your sentence and death to ensue as a result of our carefully mastered scheme we engineered against you Robert Stewart. We thought the entire show was about us. But no. Ah, no, you crafty devil Commander Robert Stewart. You had other ideas, didn't you, good copper? We thought we had everything in the bag, you know, your ruin and death trap we set up for you…but now I come to realise Robert Stewart, that the spotlight was always on you and your actions and your defence to bring about our demises. And you won Robert Stewart! You stripped us of all our plans and made us drown in the mud, the dirty slimy drowning mud of failure. All our plans, narratives and plots and schemes returned to ruinous collapse by your damn destroying, brutally wicked hands, Commander Robert Stewart. As we tried to narrate your fall, ruin, death and complete destruction, you flipped everything around, turned the tables over and checkmated each and every one of us with your damn unbeatable rulebook!

As we concocted the script and the narrative to your end, your sought-after downfall, you were always in high command and in perfect view of our deliberate brainwaves, brainstorms and schemes. And you made one final checkmate move that pulled the rug from right under our feet - and you ended us then and there in the perfect victory you delivered horrendously at our expense!

We planned your demise Robert Stewart as it was the next blockbuster cinematic movie script to hit Hollywood. We had constructed the perfect plot twist. We all thought everything was going to go our way. But you Robert Stewart…you…you…you…you had to intercept our script, and use the story we concocted for you, then flipped and thrown in our faces as forcefully as a hammer. You twisted everything that we planned for you Robert Stewart and turned it around back to us. You threw all our plans right out the fucking window. Our plans of death we had for you, you twisted that script, and instead, wrote your own narrative, that indeed turned our lives and our stories into corpses and obituaries. You really had us fooled Robert Stewart. You really masterfully turned everything around; the entire script you flipped and turned our plans for your death into our own death sentences. Now we are the laughingstocks of the entire criminal kingdom, who look at us with scorn, as failures and mugs and circus clowns and suckers. We are everything that people ridicule and say never follow what those fucking idiots tried to do. Because everything they do results in failure. They are idiots, dumb shits and fucking morons! That is what everyone is saying about us because of you Robert Stewart.

In truth, what you did is a real shock, Robert Stewart. Not that you were able to defeat us. But it's the fact that you still had breath left in you to attack us and defeat us. Because you were supposed to be gone Robert Stewart. But not even death is possible with you. Is it? Is it? Fucking is it, you scornful police commander! You cheated the entire narrative, Robert Stewart. You cheated all our concerted efforts and sent us packing into the sewer where you threw us. We really never had a chance against you, did we Robert Stewart? Here we are thinking we were the master manipulators, but it was you, Robert Stewart. You were the true devious master manipulator all along, who always carried the instruction manual of all your opponents' death-rolls. You were supposed to be wrapped in white sheets becoming a very cold corpse, Robert Stewart. By now you should have been in the mortuary. But no, Robert Stewart. It was our funerals you always scripted. You were always in command, weren't you Robert Stewart. You always knew about us and our intentions, didn't you Robert Stewart. You always have to win, don't you Robert Stewart. And now even in death, I would still be a laughingstock. The coward

Elliot Archer who took his own life to escape Robert Stewart's retributive prank and scam he has constructed against him.

But now Robert Stewart, I've come to realise that the Great Robert Stewart doesn't die because someone has narrated your funeral. No, Robert Stewart. Your tenacity and resilience don't bend to anybody's will and intentions against you. It is the rest of us who live victim to your unsurpassed all-consuming aura. Forgive me Robert Stewart for forgetting the great and almighty Robert Stewart's entire existence serves to disappoint the rest of us and our competitive streaks against you. I also forgot Robert Stewart, that you have a track record for disappointing people and their plans to have you disappear and die on cue.

But now I come to realise that as we planned for you to breathe your last breath, it was your next breath that devised the true brilliance of our eliminations. You are a haunting presence, a complete contradiction to our initial narratives about you and how things would end for you. And now as I contemplate the end of my life, I realise that all my predictions I had for your destruction and obliteration were complete and utter worthless! As worthless as you have now rendered my entire existence living in captivity inside your jailhouse custody, as is the scenario of my horrible, horrible, terrible, terrible, completely fucked and completely ruined life form as it stands tonight! I simply miscalculated you, Robert Stewart. I simply misjudged the fact that you are not like everybody else. It was a fatal flaw on my part. I made a very gross error in my judgement to think or to conveniently forget that you had the stamina, multilayered endurance, and the constitution to outlast every disaster we had in store for you, to simply remove and completely erase you. And that era of failure by my dumb ill-conceived actions is now going to cost me everything that I have left in this world. And the only thing I have left in this world is my breath, that's it. And now Robert Stewart, you have transformed all the plans we had for you, turned them around and kicked them right back in our faces, in my face. And now you will cost me that one last thing I have left - and that is my breath!

Elliot Archer had utilised a unique method of committing suicide inside his jail cell that evening. He removed both socks from his feet and forced them both remarkably inside his mouth. But found he couldn't swallow the socks in an attempt to suffocate. All in all, Elliot Archer was desperate to commit suicide right now. So, he quickly thought of a more effective solution to his troubles. He would undergo a very chilling form of suicide technique, when he began repeatedly bashing his head into the prison wall, until he achieved his desired endgame and finally collapsed onto the floor of his jail facility motionless and dead!

CHAPTER 8

Domenico Armando was conducting his baton in his right hand, but swaying both arms forcefully and intensely from side to side in perfectly-timed rhythm and rhythms, to his powerful symphonies playing, one after the other, in the background from his vinyl hi-fi record player system, equipped with a powerful amplifier and excellent quality, rather premium stereo speakers, inside his Manhattan mansion office after midnight that late evening. Domenico Armando was orchestrating his lethal dark thoughts chaotically running rampant inside his psyche, as he was constructing the death toll scenarios of his human scum fucking detestable enemies, he envisioned their torturous falls inside his mind.

Domenico Armando enjoyed his time in solitude, when he stood inside his great office space, listening to his powerful symphonies and conducting diabolical rhythms in contemplative thought, and very compelling, vigorously bitter thoughts of his next, in his mind, 'deserving targets!' In his black heart, he wanted to witness the masses of them collapsing onto the ground in bitter torments, those he blamed for plotting against his family empire dynasty, and plotting his children's deaths, and plotting against him-Domenico himself, quite personally! Domenico Armando indeed took such attacks driven against his children, his empire and against him-Domenico Armando himself, the rather foolish and daring assaults by his long list of enemies, as 'quite personal' attacks. And Domenico Armando certainly insisted on his perfectly executed, yet deliciously ruthless vengeful retaliation(s) for such, in himself, heinously wicked plots of numerous onslaughts conspired against him in the past and in the present!

Domenico Armando began fuming in rage at the thought. And he began cursing and insulting his world of piece of shit, worthless worms and contemptible swine enemies. You world of scum human filth and animal scum! Domenico thought contemptuously in his mind, furiously and angrily, diabolically and evilly. You think you can compete against me? **HUH!!!** You previously thought I was dead and done for. You world of scum, fucking scum, made the biggest mistake of your lives underestimating the all-powerful and almighty Domenico Armando! And that is a mistake that is going to cost you everything!!!

Yes. It was a fatal mistake on the part of you Scum People, obnoxious Human Race and fucked up Humankind, that will cost you your lives, your very fucking lives, and the lives of all those around you. Yes. You are going to die you disgusting vermin and filthy swine. ALL OF YOU ARE GOING TO DIE!!! You hear me? You are all dead. Dead. Dead. Dead. No one will get away with the evil things they have done, the horribly barbaric treasons they have committed against the Armando family. No one. No one of you cocky shits!

Yes. You all thought Domenico Armando was dead. Huh. Wrong. Wrong again. Because Domenico Armando was not dead. Here I am you filthy pigs! I am here. Still here, now planning my 'GREAT REVENGE' against all of you little worms of the ground!!!

I have declared my war against all my enemies! Foolish people! Complete fucking idiots! I'm about to unleash my trainwreck of disasters and catastrophes in your lives! You hear me you worms of the ground, filthy maggots and detestable human vermin! My revenge is going to be unleashed as a catastrophic storm against you ALL! My powers will mimic natural disasters. My unmatched aura will shake mountains! And my will, yes, my fucking will, will send all of you tumbling headfirst into the ground, you worthless beings! For all the crimes you have committed against the Great Domenico Armando and his beloved children, your ends are going to be black! Black like your fucking hearts! Every breath you take, and every diabolical word you speak against the Armando family - and every scheme you plot against my children - will be turned around against you all! I am going to shatter your lives from head to foot. I am going to come after you culprits and your scum children as you came after me and my beloved children! All your lives will be crushed under my feet. First, I'm going to have you cut in pieces, and then I'm going to trample what's left of you with my feet, crushing your remains into the dust. Everything you own will be burnt. I'm going to burn all your possessions into the ground. Your world as you know it will be blown up sky-high. I will torment your entire existences and send you, your children and your diabolical friends that you used to plot and scheme against my family, echoing in the torturous torments I have in store for you!

And after I have destroyed all your possessions and all your lives, it will be my name echoing through the strong winds, that blows across all corners of the world! And no one will forget the name of the Great Domenico Armando and his greatest victory, that day he overpowers and wins success and triumph against all his enemies, who will be destroyed, and their remains will be burnt to ashes across the entire world who will witness my greatest triumph of them all!

So, get ready you worthless and filthy slime. Because your ends are very near. Your extinctions are at hand. Yes. Yes indeed. Because of your actions against the Armando family and against the Armando family children of mine, I have declared my bloody war against all of you filthy human scum - and there is no turning back. There is no escaping my bloody plans of destruction, monstrously widespread destructive havoc I have planned for each and every one of you. You have unleashed the beast, the monster in me by your carelessness, foolishness and incorrectness displayed against the Armando family name. And now my actions against you will be justified. And once I begin my vendettas against all of you, there will be no force and no single power on this earth, that will be able to stop me and my calamitous, all-consuming, retaliative, brutal-and-explosive actions that I will send your way, in gigantic proportions, that you world of idiots and fools will never believe imaginable. You won't believe it's possible. But believe me when I tell you, you are going to become true believers in the true powers of Domenico Armando's destructive hands, when I declare my war against you all in extremely 'totally devastating' proportions, for all your misguided and misaligned foolish actions against me and my family name! So, get ready to die, you world of stupid numbskulls. Get ready to experience unlimited amounts of agonising pain, when I unleash, equally, unlimited amounts of havoc in your wretched lives!

You horrible people are going to suffer dearly for what you have done to my children. You are going to experience the most horribly brutal pains never experienced by any person in the history of mankind, by my powerful and mighty hands! And when you cry blood from the excruciating brutality I wreak upon all of you, you will beg the Great Domenico Armando for a mercy that will never ever be delivered upon any of you! Because hell is what you all deserve. And hell is exactly what I will declare and render upon your worthless lives!

Not only is my intention to settle scores with you scums of the human race, but my fervent intention is to also end your very fucking lives, the lives of you and all those around you, carrying your polluted genes. I will furthermore annihilate the entire existences of all those friends and acquaintances of yours you used the services, to do the Armando Family

Master, that is I, and his children the unthinkable and unforgivable disservice, by your disgusting actions, which cost me the lives of my wonderful children!

And when I am done with my revenge against all of you, there will remain not even a single trace of your existences to be found anywhere in this entire world. Because I'm going to erase the memories of your entire beings, both you and all those closest to you, who were willing participants in the crimes committed against me and my family. So, after I obliterate all of you, no one will ever remember your names, because you are going to disappear from the world's atmosphere as if you had never even existed. And that is the punishment that I have readied against all of you, for your horrible crimes against me, my family dynasty and my beloved children; my beloved children who are now dead in the ground because of you filth and scum of the human race, which lives and breathes and pollutes the entire world's atmosphere wherever you vermin lepers pass by left and the right, contaminating the entire earth's existence with your diseased beings!

I am Domenico Armando. I am the ultimate powerhouse the world has ever seen. And the war to be unleashed against you, will become my war solely and completely to dominate against the world of filthy offsprings and no-hoper arsehole people, who don't even deserve the privilege to breathe for one second longer. You swine of filth and trash are going to pay for your lies, your theft, your two-faced cowardly hypocrisies you display against everyone and everything you come into contact with, both personally and professionally, in your disgustingly perverted and undeserving lives, you do not deserve to possess in this world! No matter the cost, my path and my destiny is predetermined and my war against you is sealed. I will end all your lives on the spot, even if I have to bury alive every opposing army this world contains, who dares put their lives between me and my targets, in the process of my justified actions of eliminating all my world of bitter and despicably deplorable, worthless, useless, good-for-nothing enemies of mine! Because all my enemies are worms of the ground. They are little worms who are very soon, very soon indeed about to become extinct!!!

Yes, you world of rubbish and trash. You previously thought Domenico Armando was dead. And because you thought I was dead, you felt very safe in your little worthless worlds and nasty kingdoms to do as you please. With

Domenico Armando dead as you thought, you felt safe to toy with his children and mess with their lives and steal the royalties and block my beautiful daughter Maria's book. You also felt safe to misdiagnose, mistreat and prescribe deadly lethal medications, with catastrophically expedient deadly mortal results to my wonderful son George the Great. And you did all this, whilst wearing your false sense of securities, that Domenico Armando was dead and done for, and no one could get in your way to stop you from tormenting and torturing, ridiculing and humiliating his beloved children. But you stupid worthless useless fucking pieces of garbage of the human race were truly ignorant in your assessments, to ever underestimate the Great Almighty King Master Domenico Armando!

Just because the rest of you carry mortal beings, it does not mean that the great and powerful Domenico Armando is like you. Domenico Armando is a supreme powerhouse who is as immortal, just as his vendettas against you filthy deplorables is also eternal. Yes, my vendettas against each and every one of you is forever unending, until I truly witness all your dead corpses before my feet! And in order to crush and destroy, eliminate and kill each and every one of you, I will unleash the deadliest war against you unworthy enemies of mine! And it will be a war the world has never seen. The power of my vengeful wrath will be at such a degree, that no one in the history of mankind has witnessed the bloody massacres and excruciating pains of torments and tortures the people of the present-day will witness, through my signed declarations and practical mass killing sprees, marking my human devastations against all of you races of diseased, good-for-nothing twerps, which exist in all corners of this world at present!

Your stupid miscalculations that Domenico Armando was dead and that the darkness had consumed him forever and his eternal home was a grave, was the biggest mistake of your lives, you stupid people of this world today! You thought Domenico Armando's entire existence had disappeared and transformed to ashes and dust, just as a breeze in the wind. But you see, I have proven all of you wrong. Yes. You world of enemies of mine are so stupid, that everything you say is wrong, just like your entire existences was wrong to begin with. Because none of you ever deserved to belong in this world. All of you should never have been born in this world, FULL STOP!!! None of you had ever deserved to breathe the clean air that you undeservingly were given the privilege to experience, with your wretchedly impure and fake and phoney disgusting lives of yours, that contaminated the entire world's orbit!

You see you weak individuals of the world who are all corrupt; you people are so weak, you cannot handle any pressure. If I shake the tree where you are hanging from, you will all fall off quite easily. But what you never realised was that Domenico Armando was born in the darkness. Pressure and violence are his true name. Excruciating pressure and bloody violence are where Domenico Armando truly thrives in a world of wimps, weaklings, two-faced hypocritical cowards and worthless beings! Hell is what will consume you scum! But the very same hell that crumbles and crushes all of you, is the very same hell that Domenico Armando thrives and rises to his peak performance - and his autonomous best! You should have understood that from the beginning of your celebrations, when you thought rather stupidly, that Domenico Armando was turned to dust, previously pronounced dead inside the ground.

The pain and suffering that chokes your every breath, are the very two qualities in which Domenico Armando relishes and dominates to unquestionable power and eternal ruling in this world of cruelty and darkness, in which I currently dominate as the ultimate leader and the greatest being the world has ever witnessed! Hell is your destruction at the same time as hell is my uprising! Yes, you scum. You hear the great powerful words of Domenico Armando? Domenico Armando declares in tyrannical decrees, that all you worthless human scums are trespassing on the Great Domenico Armando's territories and domains. And thus, as a consequence, I-me-Domenico Armando declares all of you to be sentenced to your ends, to your bloody gruesome deaths on the spot right now, as I conduct my powerful symphonies in bitter unmagnanimous thoughts of all of you horrible creatures of the world!

So, get ready you world of filth and scum. Because I'm about to make you regret the day you ever crossed Domenico Armando by playing sick games with his beautiful children, Maria and George! You certainly will rue the day you ever crossed any of us! And you will curse your very fucking lives the day you ever thought your lives were safe to do as you pleased against my children, when you thought the great and almighty Domenico Armando was dead! So now that you know that I am alive, don't even think of running away. Because there is no corner of this world that you can escape from my wrath, my brutal and bloody wrath to be unleashed against each and every one of you worthless maggots. There is no one in this world who can help you, just as there is nowhere in this world that you can escape from my vengeful retaliation I will unleash against all of you, until I consume your very fucking lives; lives that you never, ever deserved to have given to you from the beginning of your worthless existences in this world! But understand one thing you creatures of the dust... As I enjoy listening to my powerful symphonies, as I'm enjoying listening to my powerful symphonies right now, I will also relish your unending screams, the beautiful sounds of your screams, once I unleash my brutal and vicious agonies, I have in the works for all of you scumbags of the world! But before you die, you prehistoric beings of abnormalities, I will confront all of you first. And you will look into my eyes, and I will enjoy watching you experience the true definition of what 'fear' really stands for, before I match your emotional pain, with the physical excruciating brutal tortures I will inflict upon all of you!

None of you are going to get away with the deaths of my beloved children Maria and George. This world of disgusting deplorables are about to experience my rage. And once the great Domenico Armando unleashes his rage against all those deserving immoral mortals of the world, everyone witnessing your ends will come to realise the true powers of Domenico Armando. And not only that will they understand, but they will come to comprehend that Domenico Armando is immortal and unbeatable by anyone and anything that exists on all four corners of the universe. Because every power in this world combined, are just slight inconveniences, who cannot even put a dent into the impenetrable fortress and the bullet-and-bombproof armour that is, Domenico Armando's eternal and indestructible presence; the unmatched presence of mine, as I will command and radiate ultimate authority and unquestionable dominating rule across the entire world, as the greatest universal leader no one has ever seen or witnessed existing in history ever before!

CHAPTER 9

Domenico Armando, as he stood on his feet holding his conductor's baton, his diabolical thoughts became more intense, his desire for unlimited painful retaliations against all his enemies in the world grew-and-expanded equally eternal in their ambitions of unquestionable and catastrophic dimensions, in the outpouring of unmatched brutalities never witnessed by any sonofabitch who undeservedly lived in this world priorly!

Domenico Armando swung his conductor's stick from side to side more fiercely, as he thought lethal plots inside his bitter maniacal mind, of severely torturing and violently killing his world of contemptibly deserving enemies. YOU WILL ALL SUFFER FOR COMING AGAINST ME! Domenico Armando's thoughts exploded inside his hideously dark mindset. You will even want to kill yourselves for ever making the biggest mistake of your lives, that most lethal error in judgement, thinking that I was ever dead to begin with. And with that horribly incorrect judgement call, that in itself stabilised your false sense of securities, to plot and scheme and commit hideous crimes against my children; now, my dearly departed children. Domenico Armando cursed such wildly vicious overtones inside his head, as he continued conducting powerfully to his equally powerful symphonies playing on his record player; its tunes blasting from connected high-volume stereo speakers.

And as Domenico Armando experienced firsthand the true magnificent essence of his powerful symphonies playing loudly inside his personal den, Master King Domenico Armando swung forcefully his conductor's baton in perfect rhythm to the mixture of the symphonies' musical instruments, high and low notes vibrating the walls of his office space that moment. And at the same time as Domenico was mesmerised in the essence of beautifully great music filling his eyes and ears and all his senses simultaneously to wonderful great heights, Domenico Armando still continued his horrendously notorious and unending, painfully vindictive rants inside his lunatic brain, he had also orchestrated in perfectly-timed motions, as equally perfect vendettas, he planned against a very long list of targets he had written in a secret journal and memorised inside his cleverly insane diabolically calculated, unlimited creative mind. NOW, you coward perpetrators against my family. I will send you to the abyss.

Through the powers of my vengeance, my retaliation and my revenge, I will throw you into that dark hole called the abyss you will not be able to avoid, because of the unmatched powers of my willpower much driven against you! And in the aftermath, when it is all over, and I have taken away all your possessions and eliminated the lives of all those around you, your family members and your sick scum friends who participated in your crimes against the Armando family, you will understand one thing: Underestimating Domenico Armando was the biggest mistake of your worthless lives! Indeed. That terrible error was truly the last and final mistake you would ever make in your despicable lives. Because crossing me and crossing my children automatically becomes the true definition of death and destruction to your lives. Your lives are going to end because of what you did in particular to my children Maria and George!!!

You made a terrible mistake by crossing my children when you thought that I, the great Domenico Armando was in the ground, finished. You stupid worthless idiots and numbskull fucking fools think you know me, the Great Domenico Armando? You think you know anything? You define everybody else by the reflection of failure and qualities of that of a mediocre loser you see every time you look at yourselves and your vile reflections in the mirror. And you base that judgement of shit you see at yourselves in the mirror, as the outlook, outcomes and sick assertions that everyone else in the world shares. This is what you incorrectly think all the time! And that, you fucking scum of the world, is the last mistake you will ever make! Because that error, was the ultimate miscalculated judgement call on your parts! That fundamental mistake will result in the end of your very fucking lives and the obliteration of all your families' lives and your friends and your colleagues, who are just as worthless as you perpetrators who committed acts of scumbaggery against me and my children!

Yes, you scumbags. You thought you had the upper hand, didn't you, when it was broadcasted that Domenico Armando was dead. You thought you were safe. You thought you had every opportunity in the world to then come after my children and inflict pain and suffering upon them. Well, now you know the truth! You know the true fate and destiny of Domenico Armando. And you will certainly know what I will do to all of you worthless people who thought you had the advantage against the Armando family.

I will spill your blood from every corner of your beings. Beginning from your heads right down to your feet, a river of blood will drain out of you. And I will personally break your bones, every bone in your bodies will be smashed to pieces. And I will truly relish in the agony and agonies of your excruciating pains I will cause each and every one of you to experience, like no one else has ever experienced such pain or torture before you, since humankind was ever created! But before you all die, I will first attack you emotionally. I will inflict much suffering in your minds, when I haunt your dreams and cause you to have devilish nightmares, every time you see my face and wake up in a pool of sweat, knowing and understanding that those members of my family you messed with, from the time of my supposed death, is going to cost you dearly! Everything that is in your possessions, will be blown to pieces. And I will drain you of your energy through my initial mental torments I inflict against you, when you see my deadly face in your dreams, those dreams that will become horrendous nightmares, when you see the picture of millions of words inscribed in my eyes, that spell everything, every bit of pain and loss I will unleash upon you all!!!

I will first drag your children and your families and all those connected to you through the dirt. I will cut off their body parts in front of all of you perpetrators of crimes and slander against me and my family tree. I will set their bodies on fire. And with large and heavy swords, I will cut their bodies in pieces before I incinerate all that remains of their existences on this earth. And I will do all these evils right in front of you perpetrators of crimes against me and my family. And once you see this, and bear witness to what I do to all those connected to you, including your scum families, you will truly wish that you were never born to experience the ultimate misery and excruciating agony I will then inflict upon all of you delinquents and filthy sewer rats, who walk around this world with fancy titles, pretending to be respectable people, but you are all in fact ignorant and not educated at all. You are the exact opposite of what you portray yourselves to the world. You are not good people as you pretend to be. You are evil wicked rubbish and garbage people, that I will throw into the bin. You are not educated. You are ignorant and uneducated scum heaps of trash and swine dung. And I will throw shit in your faces when I come after all of you, the day of your massacres! Your bloody and gruesome massacres at my hands, my will and my command! And there will be no escape from any of that! And when I attack you pigs and cows, when you think that your pain is excruciating enough, and you cannot take anymore suffering and anymore torment that I will inflict upon you, I will pour on my rage all the more viciously and brutally, beyond your expectations and limits, until I see all of you crack and crumble into the ground, all dead at my feet!!!

I have returned from the dead to take what's mine. And what is mine, is simply to witness your executions and the complete removal of all my enemies from around the world! That is what is mine! What is mine is my comeback, my victory and to witness the complete removal, obliteration and annihilations of all my enemies! What's mine is REVENGE! MY REVENGE!!!

I'm back again. You hear me, you worthless, villainous scums of the world? Domenico Armando is back for one main distinctive fundamental purpose. And that is, DEATH itself! Yes. You heard me. I am back for the outpouring of death upon all of my unworthy, disgusting and filthy cretin enemies of mine across the entire world!

My revenge, my revenge is coming! I returned from the dead to exact my

revenge! I will see the deaths of all those who crossed the Armandos. The world will see it with their own eyes. I will truly shock the world with the plans I have readied for all those who went against my family. I will make you culprits into laughingstocks. I will be the ruin of all those who participated in my children's lives coming to an end! Yes, indeed. No one can stop me, not even my greatest enemy in the world, Commander Robert Stewart!

All my enemies are going to die and no one, no force on this earth will get in my way! Yes. All those responsible for the deaths of my children are going to pay very dearly for what they did! You scumbag individuals are going to seriously regret that you were born for crossing my beautiful children Maria and George. Their torments at your hands will be your undoing, your reckoning and your excruciatingly miserable and indescribable painful ends!

And when it is time to finally kill you, after first forcing you to feel and experience the ultimate torturous agonies at my hands, I will then grind you into dust. I will make your ENTIRE existences disappear from the face of this earth, as if you pieces of vermin trash had never even existed! I will erase all traces of you, until there is nothing left that proves as evidence that you scums were even ever born into this world, to cause harm whatsoever to my children!!! So, look around you. Can you see my shadow looming ahead as a dark cloud above your heads? Can you see the walls closing in around you? Get ready. Death is upon you! I am nearby at very close proximity. I am just about to end your fucking lives once and for all!!! So, prepare, for my ultimate resolve in achieving the complete obliterations of every maggot one of you!!!